**A daring coup attempt...
A nation's bloody history...
A chance for love and glory...**

Would you dare to break all the rules?
Could you live with yourself afterwards?

Based on true events,
In a Country with No Name both horrifies and charms in its detailed account of an ambitious and desperate scheme.

A young Westerner finds himself joining a coalition of business and military interests to overthrow a government that has fallen afoul of the rich and powerful.

Author Ron Morris renews dreams of bold adventure in modern times, chronicling the thrills of life in Southeast Asia in this truly unique tale of intrigue and expats in an ancient land.

**The first book in the
"Bert Mars Adventure" series**

IN A COUNTRY WITH NO NAME

RON MORRIS

Villefort: New York

For Graham

PREFACE

There's not much time. This man is withering already, diagnosed with something fatal.

I just run, run, as I did from the PM's troops, but there is no outrunning this, I am told.

So, this is my book, my tale, never told before, as it is...

This was the time when I was young and bold. I can feel it now. I remember fondly my dumb luck and wish it would visit me again.

Ron Morris

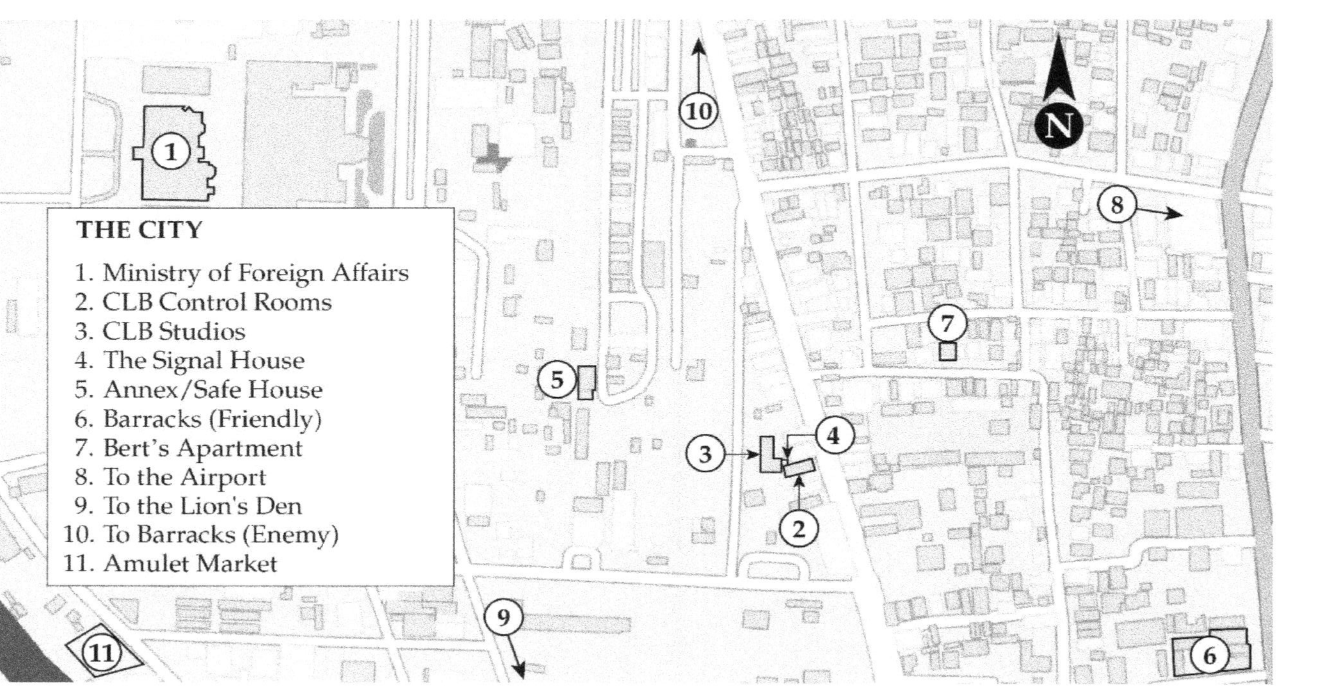

THE CITY

1. Ministry of Foreign Affairs
2. CLB Control Rooms
3. CLB Studios
4. The Signal House
5. Annex/Safe House
6. Barracks (Friendly)
7. Bert's Apartment
8. To the Airport
9. To the Lion's Den
10. To Barracks (Enemy)
11. Amulet Market

N

The characters of
In a Country with No Name

Bert Mars
   The narrator, a young, ambitious English teacher in Asia

Andrew
   Fellow teacher, a "lifer" at a Bangkok school

Noi
   Receptionist and Office Manager at CLB

Tieng
   CLB Control Room Manager

Phong
   Groundskeeper at CLB

Don & John
   American keepers of the signal house

Rangsei
   Bert's girlfriend, a general's daughter

Mike
   American "facilitator" at CLB, a former marine

Amnuay
   Managing Director of CLB

Chiang
   Well-known tycoon and owner of CLB, nicknamed "Crazy Cat"

Ganju
   Chiang's Gurkha bodyguard

Thaw Kai
   Prime Minister of the country with no name

Professor May
   A fortuneteller

PART I

1

The metal roof clattered as I barreled along. I had no time to gingerly test if the roof would hold my weight; I had to run. If I fell, I would vanish into the cracks between buildings, which were erected shoulder-to-shoulder to the horizon. I tripped several times but was always able to right myself and stay on my feet.

My footfalls echoed against the concrete all around, and the sound was so great that I wondered if people would poke their heads out of the windows to see what was going on. However, the city was loud, and my burst of rattling was just another punctuation of the day, and the sounds faded quickly, forgotten like any single strike of thunder.

The city was Bangkok. I was running away from the authorities who were checking the school where I worked. They were ensuring that all the foreign workers there were properly registered. I was not. I was ready for it, though, and I fled the building when I saw uniformed men with clipboards entering the school.

Supposedly, the authorities looked the other way and allowed English-tutoring schools to hire instructors without the proper working documents for the good of the country, since English-language proficiency was greatly needed. Thus, if a school was slow with the paperwork for getting a work permit, normally no one would care.

But my issue was that my visa had expired. Officials were always happy if one could pay the 100 baht per day overstay fine at the border and then all was forgiven. However, getting caught at the school with an expired visa could mean jail.

It did not worry me much. These were not my rules, and I was willing to be lucky. All the things I was supposed to worry about back in my home country—taxes, fines, rules, propriety—here, they were no big deal, or, as the Thais liked to say, "Never mind."

All of this was in keeping with the tenor of the times. When a police officer here stopped your car and you were able to show that you were the loyal subject of one of the big police bosses, the officer who stopped you was not indignant that he was unable to enforce the law. He just said, "Why didn't you say so? Here's my card and I would be happy to meet your police friend anytime. We should keep in touch. We could go out drinking." One could make an instant friend because everyone wanted to be part of something bigger.

I was no child of hardship. My own culture had worked hard to make sure I knew that everything was science, and nothing meant anything. And I was far away from dying and knew it. I never had to pray.

I was pure ambition, and that's what Asia was—a place where anything was possible, and we were all going to be tycoons. I was going to be a tycoon. I was going to be important.

So, on that day at the school, when the authorities arrived, I grabbed my briefcase and went out a narrow door at the back of the school on the second floor. It opened to a small porch, and I climbed over the low railing onto the metal roofs that sloped together from buildings on either side.

With each step, I tried not to plunge through the roof, which creaked under me. Hot sweat dripped off my pale forehead as every part of my being was focused on escape, and I bounded across the rooftops until I reached the street.

Then I dropped down to the pavement. If anyone had turned their head away from where I was at that instant, they would have never seen me jumping down. Looking a moment later, they would have seen a rumpled foreigner wearing his uniform of white dress shirt and dark slacks walking along in that insistent quick-paced way that Westerners always did, swinging a briefcase as if he were off to do something important. Yeah, I was just one person walking by, compact and smart, so very smart.

I had my own rules—rules for staying alive over here. Don't ride on motorcycles, don't ride in vehicles at night, and don't get on boats. Not following these things were what killed most people in these little countries. Beyond that, if something was going wrong in one country, I would just go to another, leaving the suckers behind.

After a few minutes of walking, I realized I was out of danger. Had I been caught and blacklisted for overstaying my visa and sent back to my home country like a fool, I would have been furious with myself, maybe crying over it, in private, of course. However, getting the better of the situation created an opposite elation. In this season, in this place, I could do anything. I had been tested and had come out on top again. It was the time when I, or any young man, could take a chance to do something others would never dream of. I would take a chance. A bunch of them.

I passed a temple. The temples were white-walled with red eaves suffused in gold trim. Their steep roofs looked as if they were being stretched up into the sky. The interiors were painted with the exaggerated postures of mythological creatures. Such temples were everywhere. Some said there were too many of them, most built as a sign of thankfulness and to create karma, the kind of good luck in the afterlife that only money and good works can provide. These temples were places where the infirm, the elderly, and stray dogs—all unwanted bits of life—would be abandoned.

At the temple, there was what appeared to be an old man. At least, he seemed so. He may have been the kind of man beset by some mental hardship that made him positively radiate decrepitude. He pressed a broom across the paving stones of the temple, sweeping this way and that, generating clouds of dust as he moved along, hunched and scowling.

I had seen this man when I walked by every day on the way to and from work. For no real reason, in my mind, I had named him Dang—a typical Thai name. Dang's face was usually frozen, unable to speak or change his grimaced, perhaps even bitter, expression. Sometimes, such as on this day, he stopped what he was doing and turned his entire body to me and tried to stand up straight. His face would soften and then he would struggle as if he wanted to speak. But no words ever came, and, after a moment of frustration, he went back to his ceaseless sweeping. Poor bastard.

I continued on, putting more distance between myself and the school and the insane government checks of the day. No student would question my unexplained absence from class. I was Bert Mars, but the students knew me only as "Ajarn Bert," their revered foreign teacher as were all of my kind in this country. I enjoyed no one daring to question me. No wonder Westerners liked it here. The school knew what was going on and would reschedule classes.

I went back to my apartment. I would return to school the next day and resume my teaching with a smug grin. I had been quick enough again.

Fon was there. She was my girlfriend. She was thin and athletic with a beautiful plain face—the sort of face that would grow ever more beautiful the older she became—especially to the one who loved her. I did not quite appreciate that then.

She came over sometimes. She was washing my clothes outside on my porch. She didn't question why I was back so early.

My job at the school, this room, Fon—this was my tiny place in the whole of the wide world, on the edge of the entire world which was waiting for me.

Fon had brought some cans of soda for my little fridge and some packets of potato chips. Things she thought I would like. She was a nice girl.

That night, I lay in bed watching the geckos that roamed over the walls and ceilings of buildings inside and out. They would stake their territories at porch lights, trash cans, gaps in the masonry—any place where gnats or mosquitoes or festering flying creatures would tend to be. Two or three would fight over their claim under a light and gulp down insects. Up close, one could see them hold their mouths open with their tongues extended in an animalistic exercise of intimidation. They bleated out sharp, fierce warnings to their rivals and anyone else who cared to hear them. They ran over every surface, as no smoothness, no jagged edges, no barrier delayed their search for prey.

These were common things, expected to be seen, no more remarkable than the dust that continually collects on the floor before we are born and after we have died.

Increasingly, I could not sleep. I stayed awake wondering what I could make of myself and what would become of me. I watched the geckos' patrols and the ceaseless eating that fueled their rapid movement. Their small jousting on the glass was mesmerizing.

2

"Had they only spent the bare minimum, the buildings wouldn't have been crumbling already," said Andrew, a fellow teacher, not looking up from his lesson plan.

Andrew was a "lifer." He had drifted off from his own country years ago and found himself here, in Thailand. Tee-totaling, yet licentious. Prematurely old, yet oddly immature. It forever isolated him and muted his ambition and anything he might become. He just "was," day after day, and that would never change. And he was always "Andrew." He wasn't an "Andy."

He was talking of news of a government housing development that was revealed to be vastly over-priced yet was already crumbling. It was on the front page of the newspaper I was reading.

"They would have had no trouble if they at least built it right. They won the over-bid contract," he said. "There was plenty of money to build it right."

"It was greedy for sure," I added, without emotion.

We often discussed things like this in the school break room. We both condemned corruption, like proper Westerners looking down on these tiny countries, but we were also envious, I think.

I found myself abutting great prosperity—the prosperity of an English school that could make the owner who started it rich. It made me salivate to imagine being a big boss myself instead of just the toady of one, getting by on a monthly salary.

Andrew didn't like to discuss specifics of how we might extricate ourselves from the salaried life. He had once tried to start his own school, but failed spectacularly, being raided by the police for not having the proper paperwork (and for being a foreigner, but that's another story). Now he was here, forever, broken down, just happy to have his job.

Andrew noticed I was looking over the classifieds, the job notices in the newspaper.

He told me, "Bert, you get here, and the seasons go by—they are all the same here—and others are building something back home, and you are lost here in paradise." It was said with conviction.

"I haven't given up," I said, trying to put a positive spin on his attempt to demotivate me.

"It's easy to hide away here," he said. I wasn't sure if he was warning me or advising me of a perk of the place.

"I'm not here to escape anything. I'm not running away."

"Okay," he said. "You'll see."

This stung. Andrew thought he was unique and maybe he once was. He was here long before I was. He was a cool customer, and his relaxed pessimism was a comfort in a world where everything could be ridiculed, and true riches were out of reach for those like us.

But his cynicism, repeated and repeated, made him recede into caricature. He was the dissipated expat, having allowed his life to go on as it was, lying here in the heat of Siam, year after year. I could see that, and it scared me. I resolved to keep up the job search, looking for some new opportunity, some chance, some angle.

CLB, a local television network, was planning a music video channel. They had an ad in the newspaper looking for on-air hosts to announce music videos. This is what was called "VJs" in those days. I had some experience acting and presenting (as the Brits called it) and I had the ego to do it. On-air positions were the rarest of jobs, particularly here in a foreign land where most of the work was only in the Thai language.

Everyone knew the owner of CLB. He was one of the new tycoons, Chiang, already a legend. He came from one of those average but ambitious immigrant families of Chinese who came in waves into all of these little countries. In less than a generation, they were lifted high by the tide of sudden regional prosperity. The new tycoons became the men who could never lose. Their wealth could swamp all things, could make their own country warp and bend to them.

Chiang, or "Crazy Cat" as he was nicknamed in Thai, and his sudden ventures into every industry, were not regarded with jealousy, but as the portent of how prosperous the future could be.

I made an appointment and tried out for the VJ position. They made a test video of me pretending to announce music videos. I thought I was terrible, and afterwards, I cringed just thinking about it.

But the next day, I was surprised when the network called and expressed interest. They only wanted some occasional work from me at first—afternoons and the occasional interviewing of musical acts that were coming to Thailand to perform. It was a thrilling new opportunity.

I should not have let anyone back at the school where I worked know about this. There were some weeks when I did not see the boss of the school at all, no classes were scheduled, and I just sat there. It would have been easy to get away unnoticed for the occasional VJ work at CLB.

But I told my boss at the school about this opportunity, noting that at some future unspecified date I might need some time off. He went gravely silent. He was a Thai man, a minor version of Chiang, lord of his empire of English-language tutoring schools. A nice guy, but I was foolish to reveal anything to him.

Later that day, I attended a typical staff meeting. During the meeting, the boss went on, as Thai bosses often did, about subjects like how hard he works. It was nothing out of the ordinary, but then he mentioned my request for time off to the whole group. He suddenly looked at me with tearful sincerity and asked, in front of everyone, "Bert, would you please commit to stay with the company and not take any work at the other place?"

I gasped, embarrassed and shocked, and, wanting the moment to pass by quickly, said, "Yes," adding my big fake Thai-style smile which I had learned well by then.

The boss seemed relieved, as if a great weight had been lifted from him, and then the meeting was over. This public meeting, putting me on the spot, felt insane to my Western sensibilities, but I had been around long enough to realize doing this was a sort of an honor to me, the big boss deigning to publicly admit he valued me as an employee and did not want me to leave. If I had made a scene, I would have limited my options, and one cannot challenge a Thai boss in public, no matter what he does. I just said what he wanted to hear, and he was happy to believe it. Sometimes we all are.

Andrew was there, as he always was, and made no sign as these events unfolded, but I imagined he was laughing at me, good-naturedly, inside. He was too nice to let on any of this to me and this somehow made it worse.

The meeting brought into focus how my visa and work permit allowed me to stay in this country. I had to be careful about changing jobs. I had discovered a paradise, while everyone else I knew was scraping ice off their windshields back home.

I started sneaking out to meetings at the new job at the television network, CLB. I was certain the Thai staff at the school would make sure that my absences got back to the boss.

At first, I made some excuse at the school of having to go to immigration or the bank, but finally, I just went out to CLB and said nothing.

3

I was constantly asking when the new video music channel was going to start, but it was always "in process," as the Thais would say, meaning it would happen soon, but no one knew when. The commencement of the channel was forever a month away.

Noi, the receptionist at CLB, asked probing questions of me, like where else was I working. I said I wasn't working anywhere else. I did not have a particular reason not to tell her the truth, but I had learned my lesson back at the school when I blabbed about this new job. If I had told her, "None of your business," it would have confirmed I was working elsewhere, and it would have led her to try to find out where I worked. The less she knew, the better.

Noi was the queen bee of the CLB office. She knew which employees were succeeding, which were failing, and her backdoor politicizing could propel workers to the heights of success with management or get them drummed out of the company.

She was an unmarried Thai lady, now a little too old, by Thai standards, to be married. She wore a short business-like dress every day, perhaps not becoming to her form anymore.

Often, when I arrived at CLB, Noi said I was late when I clearly was not. It was mind games, and I always pointed out that I had never been late for anything in my life. I was not sure if she actually disliked me or if perhaps this was an initiation by tempering to make sure that new hires knew that she was in charge. I tried to humor her.

I was stationed in a control room, waiting, with no duties. It was all a bit discouraging, but it was something. I just sat pondering the rows of screens showing broadcasting from the network while other Thai workers manned the consoles and lines of unintelligible Thai subtitling flashed along the bottom of the screens at impossible speeds.

The head tech guy, Tieng, was often in the control room, checking on things and sometimes adjusting something before quickly leaving. I got the sense I was making him uneasy just being there.

He had an almost feminine face and spoke with the undertone that the locals usually spoke to foreigners with. He was about as tall as I was but had a hunch in his shoulders, as if his head was pulling his body down. He was all meekness, but it was all to a purpose, as he effortlessly managed the technical staff in the company. I tried speaking with him, but he communicated with me as little as possible.

One day, Tieng looked me in the eye and then turned to several crates in the room. These were full of technical equipment. He then asked, "Do you think you could help us?" He moved his eyes to the pile of crates in the room, careful to only suggest to me his meaning, as Thais tended to do.

I understood that he needed help understanding the English-language installation instructions included with the new equipment. Luckily enough, in college, I had freelanced at a satellite broadcasting company in Los Angeles, and I had some knowledge of the technology. I began to help Tieng sort out the setup of the broadcasting equipment.

Soon, Tieng and the other tech guys treated me like one of their own. Tieng brought a guitar to work and would play 1970s Western rock songs sometimes. While we sorted out the technical equipment, he liked to talk about his favorite songs and asked me to explain the lyrics to him. He looked disappointed when I said I didn't know what the lyrics meant, as most pop song lyrics were weird poetry or nonsense. I think he thought I was lying to him when I said I did not understand them.

I started to notice how often Chiang's name was mentioned and what a presence the tycoon was at the company—as if Chiang himself was the day-to-day boss of every business in his multi-corporation empire.

CLB was expanding, and it was rumored that Chiang himself might show up at the office to do something—whatever big bosses did—give speeches, bark out orders, make things happen.

"He could show up at any time," Noi told me boastfully, as if she was on intimate terms with him. "You never know when he might arrive." Her face glowed as she spoke of him.

This reminded me how, back at the school, when the boss there showed up, it was as if a godlike presence had appeared. He would rush in, with a few people ahead of him to open doors so he need not pause, his head swiveling, judging all with a single glance. His arms would be splayed in dramatic gestures as he pointed to changes to be made, walls that needed to be torn down, groups of employees to be relocated.

Dozens of verbal dictums were made during such a visit, and no written note was made of any of them. Instead, everyone replied, "Kap pom." It was the word of assent, somewhat like "Yes," with "pom" as a suffix, denoting an extra level of servility. The boss would later wonder why only some of his orders were undertaken and the rest forgotten. Such was his fate.

I resolved not to let the opportunity at CLB go. I would show Andrew I was not stuck at the school. I wanted a new job, but I was stupidly jeopardizing my job at the school for a speculative new one. I told Tieng that I wanted a full-time job in the new subsidiary.

Tieng replied, "You don't report to me."

"Well, who should I talk to about this?"

"Maybe ask Noi," he said.

So that's what I was reduced to, asking the receptionist in this murky hierarchy about a job.

I told her I wanted to talk to someone about a full-time job and that CLB had to hire me full-time or I was out.

She said, very seriously, that she would find out about this right away. I wasn't sure if she was mocking me or not, but at least I had asked.

The next time I came into CLB, Noi proudly handed me a large envelope.

"Congratulations," she said, as if she herself were hiring me.

It contained all kinds of paperwork to fill out and an employment letter. I was stunned. I had been hired, and it was for a new subsidiary that was being set up in the neighboring country. The salary was better than what I would get paid in Bangkok and the new location was even cheaper to live in than Bangkok. It was better than I could have imagined.

The decision made, I had to resign from the school.

In the break room on the day, Andrew knew something was up. He had that power. I had told him nothing.

"You'll be back," he said, without looking at me.

I was annoyed that he had me pegged as someone stuck out here like the grizzled old-timers, like Andrew himself, and that I would return to teaching, giving up on my dream.

As if he could read my mind, he added, "It'll never happen." It was not said in malice, but as a friendly and sincere warning. I decided to ignore it.

I wondered about him, what drove him to remain here so far away from his home, like me. But we were young men and never talked directly about that, and I never did find out. Maybe he did not know either.

That day at lunch, I ate at a streetside food stall near the school that sold a Thai staple that consisted of a small fish—a mackerel—with chili sauce and vegetables.

The lady who ran the food stand was said to be a kind of witch—an older, unmarried lady who toiled away her years, the only years she had, at her food stall on the sidewalk, and that she had a special ability to choose the tastiest fish at the market. Early each morning, she would examine the mounds of fresh fish on sale to vendors and would magically be able to divine the most luscious ones by sight alone, finding those laden with the pungent eggs that the office workers eating at her food stall desired.

She always smiled at me in the Thai way that indicated interest, but also fear at what sort of creature I might be. On that day, she smiled at me as usual, and I smiled back at her. Only I knew it was my last day at the school.

I had worked up a nice resignation letter, and, the next morning, I intended to hand-deliver it to the boss's house.

As to why I was doing this without advance notice, it was because my boss, like many bosses here, was suspicious of foreigners, assuming they intended to cheat them. So even if I gave notice, I would be immediately fired, as I would no longer be under his sway. It was not uncommon for the local police to be called in to search a resigning employee's room to make sure they were not stealing secrets to start their own competing business. This was not as preposterous as it sounded, as nearly all businesses here were cynical copies of other businesses, violating intellectual property or copyrights without a thought.

When I got to the street where the boss's house was located, with resignation letter in hand, I found the road and sidewalks blocked off by police.

I began to wonder if this was a desperate sign from the universe to warn me to stay where I was. A warning to keep me in my place at the school.

After a few minutes, a police pickup truck rolled out of the street. I saw two wrapped bodies, just bodies—wrapped in white sheets in the bed of the truck. Wrapped up in the way Thais did when moving dead bodies around. No blood or flesh was visible. They were as real as anything was real. And dead. I wondered what had happened, but I knew it was the police. The police were violent and no-nonsense.

Then the road was opened, and I walked down the road. I passed a roped-off area. There were two small blobs of vivid red blood in the sun with a tiny bit of yellow fat congealing out of the redness. It seemed hardly enough for a person to die from, but I guess it was, and the police had had their justice or revenge or whatever it was.

A few police officers milled around. They were relaxed and jovial—it was always fun to kill people, I guess. As I passed by, they eyed me suspiciously. Things always happened in these places.

I made my way down the long street—more a twisting alley, so common in Bangkok—glancing over my shoulder, as I suspected that a car might be sent by Providence to knock me down, perhaps dragging me in the opposite direction. But that day, I was defying all the powers that conspired to keep me where I was. I got to the boss's house and dropped off the letter of resignation. It was done and I had proved I could not be stopped.

Does the universe help you? No! The universe throws up obstacles. I found this out once I started doing something worthwhile.

Before I left the country for the new job, there was one loose end. Fon.

On our last night together, she gave me a little amulet. It was a tiny Buddha statue, colored an unusual red color, for me to wear around my neck for luck.

"For you," she said.

"Thanks. I'll miss you."

She looked at me coolly but smiled anyway.

I am not sure what any man of my age then could have provided to a woman other than ardor—a feeling that can be mistaken for true love, commitment, or desire for a child. Fon and I had our ardor, but it was just a feeling, one of many.

As I held the blood-red amulet in my hand, on our final night together, I felt the power of that moment with her.

I grinned with the casual foolishness of a young man. Then I was analyzing to make sure I was doing the right thing—that I was making the right choice. I thought I was, but I was still sad, like when I had a dream in which I was lost.

Fon was sad too, I think, but she did not show it.

PART II

1

Sudden fate had brought me to a new land. Upon arriving, I was told that I did not have the proper sized passport photo to glue to an official paper. This issue was explained in an ominous way, in the sharp English-language tones of the immigration officer, but then, turning from grim to helpful, the officer led me to a room for errant people like me. It was a room for official photos to be taken for 20 U.S. dollars—cash only. I sensed it was a scam, since arrivals had no way of knowing if this special photo was necessary, but I went ahead and got in line for the photo. If you questioned too much in these far-off places, you would go crazy.

One person was ahead of me, a young woman having her photo taken by a uniformed policewoman. I could see the woman noticing me out of the corner of her eye. Soon she was gritting her teeth, and I could see her entire body contorting in intense emotion. Her photo was duly taken and then she rushed to a table where her carry-on bag was. She bent her head down and when she rose back up, she was wearing a proper niqab which covered her face with only her eyes showing. Her eyes were focused on me with a single-minded, glaring terror. I had seen her full face and hair in its complete nakedness. Her horror was sincere and wild, and looked right through me, on to the future, and saw as much of me as I had seen of her. She let out a sharp little shriek, like a chair being pushed across the floor, and scurried out of the room. It made me a bit sad.

For the permanent address on the immigration card, I put an old U.S. address, as this would attract fewer questions than if, as an American, I said my permanent address was in Thailand. The permanent address I wrote was one on a street I had lived on long ago: "Maplewood Avenue." It was a street name from another planet, where evenings were cool, and snow fell in the winter.

I headed into town in a dusty taxi. My new workplace, CLB International, was located on an avenue named for a dead revolutionary.

I had envisioned it located in a distant warehouse district, but it was a compound in the middle of the city, surrounded by old and new buildings and with so much bicycle and motorcycle traffic all around, it was difficult for pedestrians to cross the street.

A five-story main building stood at the front, behind large gates. This was the technical division and some offices. Beyond was a forest of towers and satellite dishes, pointing off in every direction as if looking for something to communicate with. The studios sat at the back of the compound. There was not a speck of green in the compound except for a dusty, gnarled tree in front of the main building that somehow resisted the desires of modern business to tear it down and pave it over.

On every side of the CLB compound were other compounds in the same fashion, along with some apartment buildings. Each compound was bundled together by walls of concrete blocks with bits of broken glass cemented on top as a type of makeshift barbed wire. Everything here was liable to be stolen.

The apartments were four- to five-story buildings, each balcony with freshly washed laundry fluttering in the light breeze that passed over the top of the otherwise hot city.

As was typical of business in these cities, throngs of workers, always many more than one would ever imagine could be employed to good use, teemed everywhere—from the richer, tidy office people in their white shirts to lowly laborers, continually cleaning and guarding and dozing off on broken and patched chairs.

As I entered the grounds of CLB International for the first time, one of these laborers walked up to me. He came at me from the side, shuffling up cautiously to examine me in an inquisitive manner. This man, a groundskeeper, who I would later come to know as Phong, looked me in the face with a sincere expression, which then changed to one of warning or perhaps menace. He looked me up and down, and then, in a suddenly friendly fashion, grabbed hold of the front of my white shirt and let go immediately, leaving a small oily smudge. This annoyed me, as I was used to this region's habit of respect and distance, meaning people did not customarily touch, not even for a handshake. There was probably something wrong with him, so I could not get mad. It made me laugh inwardly a little bit, considering that on the first day at my new work, my first impression would include that oily smudge on my shirt. He shuffled away in silence and I headed into the main building where I had been instructed to report to begin my new job.

There, at the reception area, was Noi. She was fussing over a mountain of papers while speaking on the phone. She looked up at me and gave the faintest nod of cold acknowledgment, as if this was another normal day and she would soon accuse me of being late again. My heart sank to see her there. I thought that I had left her far behind in Bangkok.

Noi waved me towards the back of the building, as if I would annoy her by speaking to her.

"Control room," she said curtly, pulling away from the phone for a moment.

I found several control rooms, all like the one I worked in back in Bangkok. Server racks there gathered together the innumerable cables of broadcasting. They were dark and relaxing rooms, the light of multiple screens the only illumination, most showing cameras on empty sets or color bars.

In one such room, I found Tieng. He smiled at me in his meek way as usual. Crates of electronics were stacked around the room, all well beyond my knowledge, but with Tieng I began to unbox, inventory, and set up the equipment.

Previously, the locals here had dared not touch anything until the foreign "expert"—me—had arrived.

Noi asked me to lunch that day. I was surprised but soon realized this was part of her particular Thai way of binding allies to her cause—creating familiar and informal bounds of loyalty. One would never hear, "It's not personal, it's business." In a Thai office, it was always personal. Perhaps that is true anywhere, despite what people like to say.

Having lunch meant doing what all staff did for lunch, going out to one of the open-air food stands that lined the streets and having rice with pork or fish and other local specialties, along with the obligatory glass bottle of Coke with a straw in it. I never got tired of examining the exotic rendition of the Coke logo on these bottles with the foreign-language font cleverly designed so it mimicked the unique cursive Coke logo of the original English. The bottles themselves, reused innumerable times, were always battered with the partially crushed glass turning white, standing out like diamonds.

Noi had the condescending views of the locals that Thais often harbored of their neighbors, and she complained to me of the habits of the local workers at CLB.

Despite her prejudices, the people of this land were—how did the colonialist say it—"industrious," maybe even more so than the Thais, frantic and brown in the sun as if to make up time in a world proven to be violent and unforgiving.

Whatever Noi was trying to accomplish with me with our lunch, it was probably more useful to me than it was to her. I think she was in a struggle for administrative control or influence at this new company location.

She confided that the whole company was a market grab, staking CLB's claim to the territory before anyone else could. The head company back in Thailand held the rights to broadcast the international TV content they licensed in

Thailand, but not here in this country. Yet CLB was going to broadcast here anyway. They were going to do things as the Thais always did—just do it, and, if it was successful, they could negotiate to make it legal later, assuming that all had a stake in a polite outcome. That was real capitalism, I guess.

One had to expect things would be done in this Wild West style, I thought, as I listened to Noi's frantic retelling of the company gossip while I sipped my Coke.

2

Right away, I found out I was not the only foreigner—Westerner—at CLB.

Thinking that I was the only white guy at the CLB compound had given me an admittedly false pride, thinking I was both unique and a singularly adventurous soul.

But I wasn't.

When I first saw them walking through the compound and they saw me, they were visibly shocked, halting mid-step. We said nothing to each other, but as they continued on, I heard one say to the other, "Does he work here?"

They both had that peculiar build, so broad shouldered that they seemed shorter than they actually were—the puffed-up, muscled-out men who were invariably former military. I had seen men like this serving as guards at the U.S. Embassy in Bangkok, so strange in the physiognomy as to appear a different species from the boney Thais applying for their visas and the paunchy American expats waiting to register their Thai children.

I soon discovered that these men, Don and John, worked in a metal shipping container that had been repurposed into a control room. It sat behind the tech building where I worked and was connected to a cluster of satellite dishes.

Only these two square-jawed Americans were allowed inside the shipping container. They avoided any interaction with the company staff as they passed through our building when coming or going.

Oddly enough, one of them, John, looked remarkably like me, except that he had the impossibly square and solid build of a soldier. The local staff joked that we were twins, and that I was the skinny one and he was the "fat" one—the locals in those days having yet to consider being fit and muscular as anything other than being "fat."

Around this time, I was getting the cables in the control room where I was stationed properly labeled. There were many cables no longer in use and all the unused ones had been left in place, creating a terrible and growing tangle. It was just like the electric and phone wires along every street in the city. Disused wires were never removed, but new ones were added, creating an ever-growing bundle of fraying lines.

In my efforts at identifying the cables, I happened upon those from Don and John's shipping container that came through the control room switchers, on their way to satellite dishes. I listened in on one channel, and it sounded like a phone conversation between two people in the local language.

I found several more channels of phone conversations, and others that were feeds of microphones in rooms that usually had no sounds at all, except for the occasional person walking by and speaking as they passed. Some sounded like conversations in a home. Others sounded like they were in offices where official orders were being given and acknowledged.

Tieng was often the only other person in the control room with me. Once, he noticed me listening in on the channels from the signal house.

"What are they doing?" I asked.

Tieng leaned over, and, with an uncharacteristically devilish grin, said, "Recording everything." He gestured towards the shipping container outside.

"They call it the signal house. I don't know why," he said, like he did indeed know why.

"The signal house?" I asked. "They're eavesdropping?"

"Spies," Tieng said and turned away like he had revealed a secret.

I went to the reception area and casually asked Noi about the signal house and its foreigners eavesdropping on local communications. For once, I got to her. She smiled with the Thai smile of abject horror. She said I could ask "those signal house men" anything I wanted. Then she excused herself and rushed into the bathroom to escape me. It was enjoyable to put her on the defensive for once.

Stumbling onto this was intriguing. Certainly, my level of compensation did not cover the risk of being even tangentially involved in something like this, whatever it was. As I was one of few foreigners here, I would surely be suspected, if whatever they were doing was revealed. But then, it was a chance to be part of something bigger.

I thought it was time to introduce myself to Don and John. I went out to the back of the building and knocked gently on the door of the signal house. I assumed there was a way of seeing me from inside, because, after a moment, I was shouted at by someone, John or Don, to "Go away." I knocked again, but nothing. As I was leaving the door of the signal house, I heard the muffled voice of one of them from inside say, "I can't deal with this guy."

Soon, I was summoned to the company conference room in the main studio building.

I was met by another foreigner.

"Bert? Hi, I'm Mike." He extended his hand and spoke like I needed to know what he said and was pleased to let me in on what he was saying.

He was one of the largest humans I had ever seen, tall and broad shouldered. His hands were like giant gentle catcher's mitts. He was an American, strikingly black, and as out of place here as I was.

His pleasant demeanor and apparent joy in getting to meet me conspired to make me feel delighted to meet him as well. I could tell he was the type of person who would be sent to deal with problematic people. He would charm them and warn them off asking too many questions and they would joyously agree.

We first chatted about the country and about my prior work in Bangkok with CLB.

"I was once a marine and worked at the U.S. Embassy in Bangkok," he offered.

"Yes, like Don and John?"

He seemed not to understand.

"The guys in the signal house?"

"Oh, Don and John," he replied. "Yeah, I don't know where they were posted, but yeah, they were marines too. Obviously." It was like he'd planned some other cover story but gave up. He laughed and sat back a little as if he were taking a satisfying puff on a cigar.

"So, what did you think you heard?" he said, suddenly more direct.

"It is not an issue of anything I heard," I said. "I understand that sometimes things need to be heard."

I was feeling clever. "I'm a team player. I value my job at the company," I added.

Mike tilted his head forward as if he were taking the imaginary cigar out of his mouth.

"Okay," he said, as if he were inviting me to continue.

I had something in mind. "I fully understand that we have to be smarter, over time, and pay attention. Protect freedom." By "we" I meant us—the United States. I was guessing the signal house was a listening post and acknowledging that my country stays on top by knowing more and being cleverer than other nations.

Then I added, "I would never interfere with any of that. I'm discreet. I'm sure that our country sometimes listens in, lawfully, when needed..."

Mike smiled, not altering his pleasant demeanor throughout the meeting, but he cut me off there. He went on to explain, entirely ignoring my previous comments, that the signal house was a communications relay center maintained under contract—occasionally relaying broadcasts for U.S. correspondents overseas. End of story.

He was letting me know that I was wrong about everything I thought about the signal house. He did not tell me to keep quiet; he merely seemed happy to put my concerns to rest.

However, I was not fooled and considered all this with a smile of my own. I knew and he knew.

I replied, "When I was labeling the cabling, I found all the wires from the signal house going through the tech room where I'm working. There's no reason for those lines to go through my control room. Just give me a little extra money and I'll stay late and route all of those lines directly into the signal house. No one will know."

As I made this pitch, Mike leaned back and looked intently at the ceiling, then, as I finished speaking, he looked back at me with a half nod of the head, and said, "Well, if it will keep things organized."

I nodded.

"Yes, then do it," he said.

So, it was settled. Something was settled. It was a start, but of what, I did not know.

The conversation amiably veered to other areas, such as how great it was to live here. Mike loved Asia. Loved this country. Loved the women. Loved the local beer too.

At some point, Mike started talking about how he objected to being called an African American. He said he was not African American, as he was always quick to point out to anyone who used the phrase—his family was from Jamaica. He was an American, but there was nothing African about him, he said. He was Jamaican American. He appeared happy to find another of his countrymen to confide in.

Something about both of us knowing the secret of the signal house made us brothers, complicit in the truth under the surface. Our meeting concluded and we shook hands in the boisterously friendly American way. It had been a long time since I had shaken hands with anyone, as the locals in this region preferred the distance of the *wai* or some variation thereof.

I exited to return to my work in the technical building and noticed Mike striding across the compound back to the main gate, his bearing clearly that of a military man. He strutted through the compound, towering over the local people, sticking out like a giant exclamation point. I might have guessed he would be getting into an official-looking car, but instead, he got on a startlingly small motorcycle, the old, polluting two-stroke ones that were once so common. He was several times the size of it, and he rode off with it sagging under him, all the while smiling broadly and helmetless like all the other careening motorcyclists on the streets.

This giant, radiant, lumbering man was too obvious, the least average thing one could be in this place. Yet something fishy was going on and it was being done by us—bold, exaggerated foreigners.

There once had been many of his sort here, those who knew everyone and were called upon to open doors for international companies that desired to enter the local markets otherwise controlled by clannish monopolies.

Most were also spies, who could explain what was really going on and what might likely happen. They arranged wiretapping, conspired with opposition politicians at the behest of international concerns, and kept track of weapons shipments that might enable an insurrection or tip the balance of power.

What exactly was going on in the signal house, I did not know. What I did know was that my country did not get to be the only superpower by luck. It got that way by being ruthless over a long time.

I stayed late and rerouted the cabling so it did not go through the control room boards in the tech building, but straight to the signal house. An envelope with my name on it was delivered to me at the office the next day with several hundred U.S. dollars and one 1000 Swiss franc note. It was not really a lot, but it was to me at the time. And it made me think that I was on my way to something.

3

Every apartment here was an identical cement box, and I found mine several blocks from the CLB. It was indeed an expat's room—one for the young man who arrives with a backpack. Nothing hung on its cleanly painted lime green walls. Other than a bed, the only other furniture was a cabinet. The cabinet was built into a nook where one of the giant supports of the building bulged from the wall. It reminded me I was not just in my little room, but in a hulking building being held aloft by rebar and ingenuity.

The shower did not have a heating unit for the water, a convenience I had grown used to in Thailand. Thus, the water was cold, gaspingly cold. It shook me awake each day saying, "Look where you are!"

Had I been married, my wife would have surely demanded a more proper home circumstance rather than this bare, utilitarian room, but it was all I needed for now.

I bought a small red ice bucket into which I dumped a bag of ice cubes every evening when I got back from work. This would allow me to have a cold Coke before I went to bed. That was my luxury.

I soon found a girlfriend. She was a waitress at one of the few upscale cafés in town. I ate there sometimes after work when I could no longer stomach another rice dish and wanted to have a proper hamburger.

Her name was Rangsei. She had a beautiful, pleasant face, I thought, and deeply golden-brown skin. Her shoulder-length hair fell, some in front and some in back. It was not as neatly combed as some girls would keep it. It was an endearing quirk—the girl with the tousled hair.

On our first date, we met at an outdoor art exhibition in a row of abandoned shophouses. The walls were knocked out between each building, creating a walkway through the space. All the walls had been painted with colorful graffiti—this was the art—painted by young people aping the gang graffiti of the United States, with exaggerated, hard-to-read lettering and menacing cartoon characters.

I felt slightly embarrassed by this art from my modern, crumbling world, crawling across the walls of a building in her country, but I did not say this to her.

She asked about what I had been doing back in Bangkok.

"I was working in Bangkok... at a school," I said. It was not really something to brag about. "I'm really an entrepreneur. I've got some ideas for a business someday."

I did not have any business ideas quite yet, but I was looking. I was going to be something. She pretended to be impressed.

"My father was a general," she said. "I grew up in the old mansion row downtown. It's gone now. All the houses expropriated by the government. It's too bad."

I noticed her hands were dark and wrinkled, just like every workaday girl who had to handwash her clothes and then hang them up in the punishing sun.

I wondered what kind of general her father was. Was he a real general with men to order? Or was he an honorific general, who, by dint of his tenure, eventually gained an honorary rank despite having little real power? The world was populated with such men, who wished they could command, but could not.

There was a sign noting that, when the art exhibition was over, the buildings housing it would be demolished. Every place was changing fast.

Rangsei saw the amulet that I wore around my neck. I drew it out and showed it to her.

She seemed intrigued. "This is an unusual one," she said. "Very special. Who gave it to you?"

I thought of Fon who had gifted it to me, and I thought of the last time I had seen her in Bangkok. Having the amulet connected back to a previous love hinted of my callousness. So, I stuttered a bit and only said, "I bought it at a market."

"This red color is very special," she said. "It can mean good fortune or burn you like fire."

She suddenly became serious. "Bert, do you believe in it?" she said.

"Yes," I said.

"You must respect it," she said.

"I will," I replied.

I wanted to respect her ways—different ways here. I also suspected that when I said I believed in it, it became real in my mind, becoming a comfort, even though I knew it could have no real power.

One graffiti art piece at the exhibit was a wall-sized painting of a series of ever-receding red circles within circles. We stood there beholding it importantly, like we knew what it meant.

We ended up holding hands for the first time and it was a good day.

Tieng from the tech room at CLB happened to be there at the graffiti exhibition, and we greeted each other. He had brought over his Thai girlfriend with him to the new job. She was beautiful, as these younger Thai ladies tended to be, despite having a broad, square jaw. Somehow, Tieng, with his soft features and voice, was the more feminine of the two. I marveled at how these sexy girls ended up with super-meek, baby-faced guys.

The next day, back at the control room at CLB, Tieng told me that Rangsei was one of those girls who "already looked old." This annoyed me, but Rangsei did have a face that would not change as she aged, and one could already imagine the middle-aged and old woman that she would one day become.

4

All the smaller side streets of the city were still packed mud, often with enormous twisted trees standing in the center of the road that dropped leaves and sap on everything underneath.

The sidewalks were paved with interlocking paving stones, just like in Bangkok, forever uneven and pushed up by roots. In some areas, large sections of the sidewalks had been removed and the blocks stacked up like little castles. A forever broken puzzle.

Then there were the holes, long rectangular gaps that opened to deep, dirty storm drains. They were supposed to be covered, but often the concrete slabs that were meant to cover them were broken, or perhaps some troublemaker had removed them. They were easy to fall into when it was dark.

The locals bitterly criticized this primitive lack of development that left unpaved roads and ancient trees in the center of streets. But I, perhaps seeing it through the Westerner's romanticized lens of Asian decay, thought it was spectacular.

There was so much about this country one could never really know, down dusty paths and behind concrete walls where cruel things happened. I know this to be true.

As I was leaving for lunch one day at CLB, a Westerner was waiting at the reception area. This Westerner stood impatiently, and Noi was at her desk, ignoring us both.

Although dressed in normal office clothes, I could see from his bearing and build that he was another military type like Don and John. He noticed me and said, "Well, hurry up. You've got work at the annex, asap."

I had been involved in every dish installation at the compound since I had arrived. There were several rooftop locations around town and one transmitter outside of town, but I had not been involved in working on those yet.

"You're late," he continued. Noi looked up at me with a slight smile.

"I'm not late," I said. I had no idea anyone would be waiting for me.

When she wanted to be the most irritating, Noi would slowly turn her head left and right as if saying "No" when someone was speaking to her. This was infuriating, because if I came up to ask her something, she was already shaking her head "No," as if turning me down before she heard my question.

She was doing this nodding her head thing, and I stopped, almost losing my temper, and said, "Hey, I'm not late. No one told me about this!" Then I said to the man, "Let me get some tools."

"Unsat," the man muttered to himself, but also said it so I could hear him. Noi looked very satisfied.

I got my tools and was driven over to an office building a few blocks away that I had never been to before. As far as I knew, it was used by the company for excess office space and paperwork storage. They called it the annex.

It was dim and needed a cleaning but many buildings and offices in this city were like that. It was filled with metal cabinets that lined the hallways and some of the inner rooms. All the people there were American soldier-types wearing street clothes, as if this would disguise their origins.

I was handed over to another military type once I arrived—another American—and shown up to the top floor to a series of rooms, each containing communication dishes. I was shown to one room with an unusual cone about eight feet long. The windows of the room were cemented up with concrete blocks with ornamental designs in them that left slits, so that some light filtered through. The cone was positioned to point out of the slits.

To the side on the floor was another cone, partially assembled next to a metal base.

"Get to it," I was told curtly.

"Do what? No one told me anything about this. I haven't worked on this kind of cone. Is there a manual?" I said.

The guy sighed in my face, the sigh one lets out when dealing with an incompetent. Another man was called in, a military type, obviously, and I was told that the new cone was to replace the existing one.

Like anyone with an extremely varied resume, I learned mostly on the job. So, I got to work and hooked up the remaining wiring on the new cone and some of the guys helped me lift it onto the base and secure it. If there was a special aiming procedure for the cone, I did not know what it was. I took a set of measurements based on how the existing cone was positioned and replicated this on the new cone with a few adjustments. It was quick and the men thought that my shortcut was clever.

I powered on the new cone and unhooked the old one. I walked around the front of the cone to look out the slits where the cone was pointing and one of the men, again in tones meant for an idiot, said, "Don't stand in front." I moved out of the way, as I remembered that cones and dishes like these emitted energy that could be harmful. I felt dumb but tried not to show it.

I was shown to another room, an office. This room was clean and crisply air-conditioned, but also windowless. The walls were covered with metal plates overlaid with shallow dimples. A console covered with a padded tarp was sitting at the far wall. I could tell that the console was for communications and that this room was insulated to prevent electronic eavesdropping.

A desk in the middle of the room was piled with papers and illuminated by a single lamp. A man was seated there. He was an older black man, looking down at the papers like he did not have the time to look at me. The papers showed diagrams and schematics of the cone I had just installed.

"Same target. Code: Little Man," he said to me, as if giving a command. His finger pointed to a map on the desk like I knew what he was referring to.

"D.E. It doesn't work consistently or quickly, but its untraceability is an advantage. Keep a close eye on the chatter. We need to know if he is eating what he is served and if it enhances the effect."

The man looked up at me and started a bit. Then he removed his reading glasses and focused in on me. He saw me then, really for the first time. His face went blank—expressionless for a long moment—then a look of horror, then challenge, almost violence.

I realized what had happened. I was the wrong guy. I had been mistaken for someone else at CLB. And it had to be my doppelganger John from the signal house. He was the one who was supposed to have been brought over to the annex, not me.

So, what was this cone, its radiation, and the target I had just been told about? I think I was being told about a device used to project radiation on enemies of my country—at least that is what it seemed to be.

I was not sure what was going to happen next, but I was in this lawless country, doing uncertain things for uncertain people. I stood there blankly, as if it were a cowboy showdown.

My back was to the door. While the man at the desk was momentarily paralyzed with indecision, I said the first thing that popped into my mind, "I left my tool bag outside," although I was holding the bag in my hand. I wheeled around and left the room and quickly exited the building.

I jumped into a taxi and headed back to the CLB complex, trembling a bit. Somebody had gotten sloppy out here in the sun; maybe a new guy mistook me for the person he was to bring to the annex. Then I was told something I should not know. I realized that the cone was exactly something that my deviously clever countrymen would come up with.

I found Don and John waiting for me outside the main building at CLB. They stood in front of the few stairs that went up to the entrance. Both had hands at their hips, elbows out, as if showing they were ready to fight. They were spitting mad, but oddly had little to say to me once I stood before them.

"They brought me over there," I said in my defense, anticipating their objections. "I didn't know."

Don and John glared at me. Finally, John said, "You should not have been seen going from here to there." The way he said it made me think he was mocking my nasally Midwestern voice. Maybe they were not blaming me but setting up a defense for their superiors that would deflect from whoever was responsible for this screw-up.

"I didn't know," I said again, trying to show my sincerity. "This was not my foul-up. Do you want to know your orders?" I said this cheekily, meaning I would tell them what the man at the desk had told me.

"Just keep quiet," John said, raising his finger in warning. They both walked off, almost marching.

Within moments of my returning to the control room at CLB, Mike appeared at the door.

"Here we are again. You're going to have to get you clearance soon," he said, and he was more serious in his tone than last time.

He waved Tieng out of the room, and we were alone. He sat down and was silent, creating a long dramatic pause. I felt that I did not want to wait to be lectured, so I asked, "They're irradiating people?"

Mike sighed and said, "Look, just don't ever say anything about anything you know, okay?"

"I won't," I said.

Mike was silent, blank for a moment, clearly considering. He then focused on me. He had decided how to handle this.

"You have an obligation now. You understand?" He focused all of his commanding charisma on me.

"Yes, I know," I replied. And I began to think that I wanted to be in on this.

Another thoughtful pause from Mike and then he continued. "You should be aware that... your country is often a shadow opposition in places where none can exist otherwise. And in places where the opposition is suppressed, countering that sometimes takes... force."

"And they're poisoning too?" I added, perhaps a bit too eagerly.

Mike sighed. "I will speak now, not attesting to the truth of anything, but after this, it is never spoken of again, okay?"

"Okay," I said.

He leaned forward slightly. "They triangulate those dishes—those cones—and cook 'em over time. Directed energy. They can scramble their brains. Or give 'em cancer.

The process can be helped along by adding various additives to a person's meals. Not poisons—like B vitamins. Nothing out of the ordinary."

I thought of the many enemies of my country who had died in their prime of a sudden cancer or some other ailment. Yes, the enemies of my nation were always ailing.

"So, are we spies?" I asked.

"You better hope not... and never say so!" He was his jovial self again. "Spies serve time for drugs or some other offence because neither side wants to lose face admitting they are spies. Then they are traded back to their home countries."

I went silent. I knew there were always consequences when one takes a chance.

"Hey, don't worry. It's okay. If you want to go back, we'll ship you back to Bangkok. But you've had the white boy's luck so far!" He laughed. "And you checked out okay."

I assume he had done some sort of security check on my background, but I must have looked like I was pondering this, because he continued.

"It's important, okay? Just don't say anything, anything at all. Don't brag, nothing, and you'll be okay."

"Okay," I said and nodded my head and pushed my chair back a bit as if he did not have to say more.

We stood up and shook hands in a hearty way, maybe like men who had seen battle and terrible things.

"Never speak of this," he said again in the friendliest manner.

"I won't," I said.

He left and I sat alone in the control room with monitors showing broadcasts from various studios in the complex.

I had once known a lady with cancer. I visited her at her hospital bed. She was a reporter, unfriendly to her corrupt government that was an ally to my nation. She had suddenly come down with the disease. It made me wonder.

I thought of when dictators, unfavorable to my country, fortuitously died. I wondered.

Irradiating people over time. It brought home the ruthlessness of the world. The real world. The magic of science killing you. I considered if now, I would be cooked by radiation in my little control room at CLB or at my shabby apartment after work, to be discarded once I had played some role. It would be cruel and random, something done to me by the secret part of some crafty empire.

It had been an unexpected day, and I did not want to think about it anymore.

PART III

1

Long before he arrived, the staff at CLB was abuzz. Chiang was coming to visit. The biggest of all the big men from this world that I lived in, and the one who paid my salary, could appear at any time. No one knew exactly when he would appear, but his forward security men had already walked through the compound, accompanied by local soldiers. They barreled into my section of the technical building, speaking in concerned tones, noting details on clipboards.

I could tell these soldiers were "our" soldiers by the white unit pin they wore. This designated them as a certain faction that controlled a nearby base friendly to CLB and presumably Chiang.

Each military base in the country was aligned to a political party or business entity. Other factions associated with the prime minister or coalition political parties had different unit pin colors such as brown and maroon.

The men looked right through everyone in the office, particularly me, with an analytic stare, as if the people, the walls, and the furniture were not real, but simply geometric shapes to be evaluated.

One of the men accompanying them was clearly in charge. He was tall and thin, dressed in a white shirt and tie. His expression was all business, the kind of look that made the rank-and-file staff stare down intently at their work and try to look busy as he passed by. He was smoking a cigarette distractedly, something that people used to do in places of work. Where he gestured, whiffs of smoke jumped out from his hand. He looked like the sort of person who had many things under his purview. He gave orders and pointed here and there, while others with him translated from his Thai language into the local language for the soldiers.

His head snapped in my direction, and he spotted me. He came over and looked at me inquisitively, as if he were studying a peculiar bird that had alighted on his property and that pleased him. He introduced himself.

"I'm Amnuay," he said, as if I should be impressed to meet him.

"Nice to meet you," I replied. "I'm Bert Mars."

He ignored my name, but instead was watching for my expression showing I was honored to meet him. Then he said, "How are you getting on here?"

"I really like it." There was nothing to our conversation and I did not even know who he was, other than he was someone important.

"So, you... just work in here. The control room?"

"Yes," I said.

Then he said, almost to himself, "Okay. That's great." He suddenly was extremely pleased with me. Maybe Mike had told him who I was.

I thanked Amnuay and he nodded and returned to the security detail that was moving out of the room.

I asked Tieng about Amnuay. Tieng was genuinely shocked at my question. "That's the MD," he said, meaning Amnuay was the Managing Director of CLB International.

"He doesn't like them," Tieng added, gesturing in the direction of the signal house, but he would not explain more. So, the subterfuge of Don and John's snooping that the CLB had to cooperate with was not okay with the MD. It was an interesting place I found myself in.

News soon filtered through the office that Chiang was not coming to the CLB compound after all, but to the nearby friendly military base.

Noi made her way through the building, summoning all to assemble in front of the compound, as we were going to be bussed off to meet the boss. Eight vans, brand new, with darkened windows and icy-cold air conditioning, were to drive the staff over to the base.

The base we arrived at was in the center of the city, not far from the CLB compound. Such military bases, located in urban areas, were a feature across the region, important tools to conduct coups or otherwise bring pressure against governments right in the heart of their own capitals. It was located on a city block with gates on two sides out to the streets on the boundaries.

Inside were lines of armored personnel carriers or APCs. All around the base was festive bunting, as was the tradition, pinned up for the arrival of Chiang. On one side of the base was a six-story building—a general, multi-purpose kind for bureaucracy—with deeply inset windows to protect from the sun. Air conditioners chugged away on concrete eaves hanging from each floor of the building. The bottom floor was where we were being herded. It was a large meeting hall with rows of tables and chairs.

Some employees from CLB were already standing outside of the hall, anxious to get inside where the air-conditioning was. From the corner of my eye, I noticed Phong, the shambling groundskeeper from CLB. He was wearing a somewhat disheveled soldier's uniform and scowled at me, before returning to a blank expression. He vanished into the throng of CLB employees and soldiers waiting to be shown in.

Once inside, there was a stage and podium where Chiang would give his speech. The CLB logo was proudly displayed on the front of the podium.

I had been thinking what I would say to Chiang in the off chance I could meet him. I happily noted that Don and John were not there. I was the only stark white face in the room and that would surely make me stand out.

Everyone was seated, and, moments later, Chiang appeared. He had a reputation—unusual in that part of the world—for extreme punctuality. This left his countrymen stunned and perhaps even insulted that an event would begin on time.

Chiang was a square-headed man with a flat smooth face, probably in his late 50s by now. But it was hard to tell. Perhaps it was weather and genetics, but the people where I had come from, my own kind, always looked a decade older than their actual age. By the time we reached our 50s, we were wrinkled indeed. But Chiang looked young or perhaps ageless.

He was far away on the stage, and I was a remote audience member. It was as if I were seeing him on TV again.

Chiang made a short speech in English, all generalized statements about CLB's new business activities and what they meant for the prosperity of the nation. Then it was over. Everyone stood and chatted as we began to file out of the hall.

Out of nowhere, a huge hand fell upon my shoulder and turned me around. It was Mike. He guided me over, right into the scrum of security men and then face-to-face with Chiang, the boss himself.

Chiang radiated his power to those around him—sycophants, true believers, loyalists, and opportunists. Amnuay was by his side, introducing Chiang to various attendees. Chiang greeted them, probably feigning interest, as a good politician does.

Around Chiang were several security men. One was a fierce-looking man who I later learned was a Gurkha. His face was tattooed—the sort of blurry, figurative shapes that looked like they were applied long ago and had slowly spread out over a life of continual readiness. He glared at me as if to show he could spring into action to protect Chiang if necessary.

Mike interrupted Amnuay's introductions with a smile. It made me think Mike could get away with anything and made me think I could get away with anything too.

"This is who I told you about," he said to Chiang, as the other men fell silent and everyone looked at me.

I *waied* Chiang in the Thai way, but he scoffed good naturedly and instead extended his hand for me to shake.

He looked me in the eye and said, "I'm glad you're with us." He turned to Mike and said, "Be sure he is there."

"I will," said Mike.

And that was it. Chiang moved on to speaking to someone else in Thai after returning the person's gentle Thai *wai*. Yes, as was said about Chiang, he was both Westernized when speaking in English and then could shift gears to different tonalities and physical cues when conversing in his own language.

Then his group, including Mike, moved away. A group of locals behind me flooded in to replace them. I was back, part of the worker bees again, after a brief moment in the sun.

But I had met Chiang!

Tieng was by my side, expressionless. "I met him," I said excitedly. Tieng said nothing and looked bored, but I had started to suspect that he often hid what he really thought.

Afterwards, I went over the events of the meeting in my mind—what I should have said to Chiang or what I could say next time to him.

And Mike—he had an encouraging aspect that made me want to be part of the team and think that I was doing good. It also made me consider the duplicity of what was going on and what I was doing in the middle, or at least the edges, of it.

When I was back in America, I had worked in a computer repair shop that was forever on the edge of bankruptcy. The boss there had an affirming air that always made me think that I was doing a great job, and that the business was heading in the right direction, despite evidence to the contrary. Then one day, I showed up for work and the business had closed—the boss had vanished, along with my last paycheck.

I scanned for duplicity in Mike's encouragement but found none. I knew that my time in this place would lead to something great. I was certain of it.

2

Late in the afternoon, I was summoned to Noi's desk at the reception area. She was reading a folded paper as I walked up. She made me wait a moment and then refolded it and handed it to me.

"You've been invited," she said.

I opened it. It was a note from Amnuay. I was invited to attend a formal reception that night for Chiang at the compound of Prime Minister Thaw Kai.

So, Noi had been reading the note to me from Amnuay and did not care that I knew it. I was not mad. In a way, I was happy she knew. She would know I was not to be trifled with.

"You can bring a friend," she said, repeating information on the note that said I could bring someone.

"Or a girlfriend. She'll be impressed," Noi said.

It crossed my mind that Noi might be the one who wanted to go with me. I knew better than to get tangled up with her.

I offhandedly said, "Yes."

She looked at me blankly as I turned and walked back to the control room.

I had no idea if she knew I had met Chiang. I had not seen her at the military base. I could not tell if she was impressed or resentful, but this invite should show her the circles I was moving in.

I immediately called Rangsei to tell her of the plans and ask her to come with me and be ready at 7 pm at my place, when a van would take us to the prime minister's residence. I was hopeful of impressing her, but, like Noi, Rangsei betrayed little emotion. She calmly accepted my invitation. I was getting used to this.

This feting by the Prime Minister underlined Chiang's importance. It was a thrilling eventuality for Thais that their businessmen could be treated as an equal to the prime minister of a neighboring country. These Thai businessmen styled themselves as big brothers, all the while nursing traditional prejudices about the true humanity of men of different cultures.

That evening in my apartment, I turned on the television. There was Prime Minister Thaw Kai himself giving a speech. Interestingly, the speech was subtitled in English. The English was all weird fungible text expressing something about self-determination couched in the nation's fretful history, but the real meaning was lost on me, even in English.

Prime Minister Thaw Kai styled himself a brave man who transcended history, always and ever a survivor. He was brutally cruel when he needed to be, just as I had heard Chiang was, and he was someone who was never seen to lose, also like Chiang. He boldly held on to power with a confidence that annoyed Western nations who thought that their disapproval should unnerve his regime.

His nation contained too much history. It had been trod upon for too long. Its soil had become the most infinitesimal powder. Its mysterious past could no longer be understood. Its vast ruins had no original names—all lost, their glorious history now only assumed. The rocks themselves, hewn by unknown seigniory, worn away as if eroded by water. The nation had been stolen over and over, even its name changed, by those who coveted it.

But it was Thaw Kai's now. He had eclipsed it. It was all his. And I was going to his party as the guest of Chiang himself. It was beyond all my expectations.

As I watched Thaw Kai's speech, I prepared my best pair of blue slacks, picking one that was the least faded. Wearing faded clothing marked one as a drone who worked each day for a meager salary, not daring to buy new clothes until the very last of their color had vanished. Hand-washings of clothes by old washer women and then their hanging in the brutal sunlight quickly dimmed every color.

Thus, I held back one set of work pants for special occasions so they would not be subject to the repeated washings and fading.

I shined my dusty black work shoes and tried to iron the creases from my best white dress shirt. I was terrible at ironing, and, in the end, all of the wrinkles reappeared.

I sat on my little porch, craning my head over the edge of the solid cement balcony rail to catch a glimpse of the people still coming home, stopping to buy sacks of food to eat before heading to apartments just like mine, and then ironing their shirts just like I was doing.

Thinking this made me happy that I was going to do something elite. I was going to a party at the prime minister's house. There had to be some opportunities to be had at this level and I was already there, in just a few short weeks of living here. I was pleased with myself.

The sun was setting on this day, the only day of its kind there was, and I was getting excited. As the skies slowly darkened, lights came on in the town, one or two here, one or two there. A van, sent for me and Rangsei, who would arrive soon, and bring us to the party.

I went downstairs to the lobby of the building, and she was there, wearing a red silk wraparound dress befitting the reception we were going to attend. It was a finely threaded garment that, the closer one looked, the more intricate its design. I could not help thinking of my own grand future with her.

3

Young men farming the land watched as our van rushed by. Rangsei and I sat close together as we moved through the countryside. It was growing dark, red sunset tinting the fields of emerald-green rice and the occasional buffalo tended by either a very young boy or a very old man. And there were legions of large wooden water wheels, each slowly turning, delivering water endlessly to the fields.

"My grandfather had a farm like that," Rangsei said. "He died during the regime. He was a good man," she said wistfully. "I remember him a little."

"I never knew my grandfather," I said. "He worked in insurance. He died of a heart attack in his fifties."

As our van passed, too close and too fast, an old man tending a buffalo stopped and took off his hat, contemplating us as we roared by. This world has both barefoot men beating buffalos in the dust and vehicles carrying alien men to places that few could ever go. Most men were linked to their small towns, fated to die young.

We soon entered the gates of the Lion's Den, military base and headquarters of the nation's strongman, Prime Minister Thaw Kai. It was much like the CLB compound—a collection of various structures, scattered within a high-walled enclosure.

Inside, we alighted at a grand hall where a reception for Chiang was being held. The hall was several stories tall with

Corinthian-style columns holding up an overhang covering the entrance. Rangsei was impressed. I was too.

Moments after the van pulled away, a Mercedes arrived. I had never seen these cars on the streets of the city in this country, nor had I ever seen people like those who exited the vehicle: an old pale-skinned Chinese-looking man with a top hat, and his wife, face powdered white and sporting a towering bouffant hairdo.

Next to roll up was a red Ferrari. A young man in a flashy hoodie covered with Run DMC logos got out.

"Corruption," Rangsei whispered to me.

"What kind of business would it take to get that much?" I said.

"Run your own country," she replied. "Or go to the West."

"I never knew people who had money like this," I said. "Just those that had it and spent it. Where I come from, people don't want money. They just want to spend money."

I thought that knowing this made me different. I thought of the lives of my countrymen, working nine to five for the best years of their lives, when there are places like this where money flowed, and big men take a cut of everything.

We entered the hall. Inside, it was high ceilings and elegantly attired locals—coiffed hair, shiny shoes, glittery jewelry.

Rangsei's tousled hair contrasted with the other women who were older with big hairdos and white-powdered makeup on their great round faces, a different species from Rangsei. One walked past and scowled reproachfully at her.

"She thinks I'm one of their husband's minor wives," Rangsei said. "Brought here by a foreigner as a ruse so that I may enjoy the party. They will wonder which of their husbands I belong to." This amused her and she chuckled, taking a glass of champagne from a passing tray.

The language here was still entirely unintelligible to me. It was relentless in the way it was spoken, making it a tickertape: dispensing stock numbers, gossip, business ideas, all off limits.

Then a crowd of men moved past us with Amnuay in the lead and then he moved aside, and Chiang was there. We all introduced ourselves, Chiang diplomatically acknowledging he recalled me from before, probably making me appear consequential to the other men.

I spoke of my days as a teacher, now past, I thought, back in Bangkok, and, upon hearing the name of the school, Chiang immediately said, "Yes, I went there in my youth. I remember the professor well. He was one of the most capable teachers. I did not know he was still teaching."

"He is still going strong," I said.

Chiang was speaking of the owner of the school where I had worked. My old boss at the school would have been proud to know Chiang knew who he was.

"I credit him with getting me into university." Chiang continued. "I'm so happy to hear he is well and teaching."

I was finally having a conversation with Chiang himself. Nothing of importance was said—it was chit chat—but I could tell he had the politician's talent for creating the impression that he had an intense interest in who he was talking to.

Rangsei was politely speaking with the female in the group—one of the tall-haired matronly ladies. I noted how Rangsei must have appeared common with her natural flowing hair and no makeup—a regular, and, I thought, beautiful, city girl. It made me cherish her.

Eventually, Chiang began speaking with someone else and Amnuay asked me polite questions about my background.

I mentioned I was from the United States and that I had some background in communications. I could detect Amnuay sniff a bit with disapproval at the mention of the U.S.

"Your country has bases everywhere. Military bases," he said. "Are there any countries with bases inside your country?"

"Of course not," I said.

"Your country just does what it wants because it can, yes?"

"I suppose," I replied, being careful not to smirk.

"We can't fly to your country and run things there," he continued. "It's not even a dream we have. Yet."

Ah, a Thai with ambition, I thought. It was all a weird boast, the same ambition that caused Thai businesses like the CLB to stake their claims in neighboring countries.

"Someday," I said, shaking my head in approval. "I don't care one way or another. It's not my decision where my country intervenes. And I suppose there's plenty of reasons not to like the U.S."

Amnuay thought and decided he liked my answer. Maybe I had passed a test.

"I wasn't sure about you, as your involvement was with communications." I thought he meant Don and John and the signal house.

"Seems you are independent," he said. "Just make sure they don't focus on me." He smiled, like it was a great joke. "Oh, I'm aware of it," he continued, smiling.

I realized he was referring to the irradiating cone that I had worked on at the annex.

"Just make sure, if anyone has to know, that we at the CLB always cooperate. Chiang always cooperates. There's no need for any... you know."

"I'm not involved with that," I said. "It was an accident I was there. I'm sure Mike can tell you. Like you said, I'm independent."

As I spoke with Amnuay, he was probing who I was, yet, at the same time, he had a glibness that told me he might not back me up in a pinch. Funny how some people cannot hide this trait.

Why was I here at all? I was less than nobody, really. I was a lowly English teacher from Bangkok scratching for a fortune, but it was true that these countries placed a special value on Westerners, and even back in Thailand, I found myself invited to gatherings for no real reason I could divine. It seemed I was an ambassador from a remote "advanced" country that had knowledge that these smaller countries required. Not that anything specific was ever asked of me, except what I thought of their country, and the answer was always that I loved it, as if I were a validating status symbol.

The conversations in the group I was in suddenly ended, as something was said that I did not understand. Then the men of the group started to move towards the front entrance of the hall.

In an instant, I decided to go along with them. I figured I would just leave if someone told me to.

Rangsei glanced at me from where she remained chatting, and I followed Chiang, Amnuay and his other aides from Thailand.

We moved out of the building and over towards the nearby gates of Thaw Kai's residence. Rearing lions and their standards loomed over us from the gates. These were Thaw Kai's personal insignia. They were dabbed with gold leaf, as was the custom for conferring blessings on a protective image.

Beyond the gates, Thaw Kai's house was typical of the time for the biggest of men—a pastiche of Italian- and modern-style, with big Corinthian pillars at the entrance. Behind the house arose a forest of huge antennas, key to Thaw Kai's control over the military and his nation.

We removed our shoes, as was the custom, even Chiang, and entered the house.

It was dim inside. The entry hall was surprisingly modest, and a marble staircase led up on the right to warm light on the second floor. At the base of the staircase was a statue of smiling Cupid, posed so it looked as if it could start moving at any moment. Its dead white eyes were unsettling, and I thought it must be scary to have to pass it in the night.

We all flowed up the staircase, its banisters and balustrades designed in art nouveau fashion with gentle spongy edges that referenced leaves in the forest.

Upstairs, the hallway was as wide as the rooms that stood off on either side. The floor was a rich wood that felt cool and soft underfoot, as if one could lie down and sleep on it.

We entered Thaw Kai's office. It was large, but not huge, with a wide desk about eight feet long.

Moments after we entered, Thaw Kai came in through a door, without looking at or acknowledging us.

For the instant the door was open, I saw that the room on the other side was covered with the same dimpled metal plates that were at the annex where I had been mistaken for John. It was Thaw Kai's secure communications room. I could not imagine my good fortune at being here at the nexus of power.

Thaw Kai walked to a low cabinet along the back wall and placed some papers on a stack there. He was complete confidence, the back of this thinning head of hair to us. No power could resist him in this place, his domain. He turned towards us, acknowledging us with a slight nod of the head, and moved to his desk, still standing.

Thaw Kai distractedly examined some papers on the desk as if to show he need not put on any airs for the people before him. Suddenly, he ceased to be the prime minister and looked like an impatient functionary in an office, slightly annoyed at those it was his duty to meet.

From the front, his jet-black hair looked shiny and too long and pulled to the side. His mouthful of crooked teeth looked like fangs. His skin was pock-marked and the deep, dull brown that one gets from a life of not being afraid of being out in the sun. He had been through it all and was now the lord of everything he saw.

Thaw Kai rounded the desk and shook hands with Chiang saying, "Nice to see you," with Chiang replying in kind. Then, skipping Amnuay, Thaw Kai pushed through the group to me, the outsider in the group, which he must have picked out when first seeing us. I detected that Chiang was mildly surprised that I was there.

Amnuay said something to Thaw Kai in the local language, introducing me. Thaw Kai made a sound with his mouth like a clack and poked his head towards me, his teeth jutting like little irregular knives. He was a man scared of foreigners in general, but not at all scared of confronting them, if necessary, I thought. He took my hand in a flat handshake, like those not used to shaking hands, then put his other hand on top of mine for a moment, then slid his hand quickly off, turned his back to me and walked to his seat at the desk. He was through with me. He was wearing shoes while we all stood there in our socks.

I noticed there were no chairs for us. It created a shiver of excitement in me as I realized that Chiang, the billionaire who bestrode two nations, was going to be made to stand for whatever this was to be.

Then Thaw Kai spoke in clear English, and I was taken aback at his suddenness.

"These negotiations are ongoing," he said. It was not clear whether this was a question or a statement, but he was looking confidently, almost confrontationally, at Chiang. This was a too quick and too bold statement at the very beginning of a friendly meeting.

Chiang took a breath and replied, speaking clearly in English as well. "The agreement has already been agreed upon. It's a good agreement, it's legal, and there are benefits for all."

This "benefits for all" part was something I recognized from Thai culture, where it was a sideways method of saying that there was plenty of room for graft and kickbacks so that everyone involved could be satisfied that they were getting some profit from the deal. However, I had never heard it said in business dealings like this so openly.

Thaw Kai then shook his head vigorously and emphatically said, "No, no." This direct speech was uncommon, where indirect utterances left room for all to save face. "We have said there will be a negotiation," Thaw Kai said.

Chiang replied, "Brother, let's let Amnuay handle it."

I assumed what I was hearing was that there was an existing agreement, no doubt for the network I worked for, for which there was pressure to renegotiate. By pawning this off to Amnuay, it might be a way of drawing out and stalling any change. Thais were expert at this. Amnuay beamed, looking both capable and trustworthy.

"It's not like that, my brother," Thaw Kai said, touching the documents on his desk as if to straighten them a bit. "You've come here to deal with this, and I've come here to deal with this." Then taking on a slightly more conciliatory tone, he said, "You have to understand the condition of the international commitment here. The deal you have is not the type that is acceptable to them. It's not an international standard."

He then added, "It's not something we have control over." This was certainly a concession for the prime minister to admit that he, the ultimate power of the land, did not have control over something, and then also using the word "we" instead of "I," meaning his realm was under the suzerainty of some other force.

"The U.N.—they are in control. For now," he added.

"The present arrangement is legal, and it should stay," said Chiang, pressing his own point. "There's no reason for it to be changed now. We should stick with it. It's good for all parties."

"Yes, we will find a negotiation," Thaw Kai said, fairly spitting out the words. He was as crass and ugly as Chiang was Westernized and refined. But both were steely and capable. Chiang has his billions, and Thaw Kai possessed an entire nation.

Then a moment of silence. Thaw Kai tilted back his head as if to signal the meeting was at an end. Chiang audibly sighed. It was clear both sides had made their point and nothing more would be decided now. I could see what had happened. Instead of some congratulatory reception for Chiang, Thaw Kai had made Chiang walk over to his otherwise darkened house, remove his shoes, and present himself at his desk. Everyone could sense Chiang had not got what he had wanted.

Thaw Kai and Chiang approached each other. Now was the parting, marked by the prayer-like gesture of the hands, the *wai*. Both started to *wai*, but the inferior was supposed to *wai* first and the superior a fraction after, thus making clear the proper status of each.

At times, this was turned on its head, as a bigger man, when meeting another, wished to feign he was the inferior as a sop to the other, a sort of flattery. So, both Chiang and Thaw Kai rushed to *wai* first, to show a fake deference, a voluntary abasement to the other, but both noticed what the other was doing, and both stopped mid-*wai* awkwardly. Then Thaw Kai reached out his hand to Chiang for another flat handshake. They held each other's hands, palm over palm, in their burlesque of the Westerner's greeting.

I detected Thaw Kai trying to pull away, but Chiang was showing he was Thaw Kai's equal—and surely Thaw Kai realized this and it gnawed at him: the head of a nation kowtowing to a foreign businessman, and, even worse, to a Thai. Then it was over. They separated and all *waied* Thaw Kai and he *waied* back and we flowed out of the room.

It was an elating evening. It was elating to think I could see into something that was going on at the highest levels—a tussle between men who were actually consequential. It occurred to me that perhaps I had never met a consequential man before. I pondered my good fortune.

Rangsei was waiting in the hall, now standing chatting amiably with a clutch of the bouffant-haired women, all now beaming at her. I walked over and she took me by the arm in front of the women and gave her goodbyes to them. We walked out into the night air, still rather hot even now.

"I had to make sure they knew I was with you for real," she said. "They are happy now. I don't want to get a face full of acid tomorrow." She laughed as if this was amusing.

Yeah, that was something that happened here when the spurned older wife takes revenge on her husband's new young girlfriend. "They know you're my boyfriend," she said, smiling.

We had actually not used that term before. I could not help smiling too.

We returned to the city, and she came upstairs to my room. She had never been there before. She moved slowly, looking here and there, as if discoveries were to be made from examining the generic things I had accumulated. There was grace in her movements, deliberate and flowing, poised and genuine. The more I was around her, the less plain she became.

"I wanted to see where you lived," she said. Her voice was smooth and modulated and continual, as if it were a line in a song.

"Okay," I said, trying to think of something else to say.

She peered at the paperback books I had bought from the used bookstore down the street, as if they might impart something important about my character. But they did not. I could not even remember what they were about. They were the same clichéd adventure stories that were told over and over with different covers.

She completed her circuit of the room and we both stood, facing each other. She looked for a place to sit, and, before I could offer her anything, she sat down on the bed. This is good, I thought to myself. Everything was fortunate for me that day. I noticed her hair. It was always tousled, as if she should have combed it, yet it was perfectly out of place.

We moved closer, then, our heads closer than normal, then closer, then the first kiss. Something like this was happening.

I noticed what she was, her characteristics—her burnished brown skin, the lines around her eyes, the languid walking like a staid woman and then the quick excited movements of a girl. Not special, but also unique, some genuine thing unto herself.

Then she pulled back, her frame stiffened, and a serious look crossed her face for an instant, and then we were close together again, in some instinctual ritual of kissing.

She placed her hand on the red amulet that I wore. It was clearly visible through the outline of my shirt. "Not many Westerners are as superstitious as you are," she said, and laughed. The laugh was strange and broke the spell that she had been creating. Like she was laughing at me.

She stood up and took a step towards the door.

"Do you want to go to the waterfalls this weekend?" she said. "We'd come back Sunday night."

I realized this would mean at least one night staying overnight, maybe two.

"It's a holiday time, so the buses will be full by then, but I can buy the tickets now, if you want," she continued.

I said, "Yes, let's go."

She flowed to the door, telling me we would leave Friday on the bus from the central terminal. Then she and her tousled hair were gone for the night.

After my triumph of being at the Lion's Den, of meeting Chiang and Thaw Kai, I had to brag. The next day, I called my old boss at the school back in Thailand. I had not wanted to think about my past life until I had something spectacular going, and once I did, I wanted to tell my old boss of my good luck. I told him of meeting Chiang and of Chiang knowing who he was.

"You should come over for a holiday. It's great here. It's a fantastic place."

"Oh?" he said. It was the best Thai non-answer.

"Yes. I'll show you and your family around. It's an interesting place with a lot of history and interesting things to see and do."

"Ahhhh," he said. It was another expression meant to be a non-answer. I asked him how things were there, and he said they were good.

I realized he was unimpressed that Chiang knew him or perhaps he did not believe me. I thought I knew him well, but I could see I was now to be held at arm's length, another impossibly peculiar foreigner. It made me sad because he was a nice guy, but I knew there was little trust between him and people who were not his employees. I had abandoned his empire. He did not know who I was anymore.

The next day at lunch, I was eating at a food cart near CLB. Mike roared up on his motorcycle with a local lady on the back. He was dressed in casual attire, shorts and a huge Bermuda shirt flapping in the breeze. It was Friday, and, like all management types, his weekend was starting early.

He saw me and came to a quick stop.

"How was the show?" he said. For a moment I did not know what he was getting at, but then I realized he meant Thaw Kai's party. Then it occurred to me that Mike had not been there.

"It was wild," I said calmly, trying to show I was as smooth and casual as he was, but I wanted to be congratulated for how bold I was and my good fortune. "I met the PM at his house."

Mike nodded. "Interesting times. Have a good weekend," he said and careened away, as if he already knew what had happened. He was a giant on a tiny motorcycle with a tiny local lady on the back, grinning almost unbearably.

4

Half-past five on Saturday morning was too early, but Rangsei showed up at my door on time for our trip, saying, "Did I come too early?" I did not question her expectant wide eyes and soft voice. We boarded a provincial bus, and it took us far out of town.

"You will like it there," Rangsei kept telling me. I was already sure I would.

The bus deposited us at the base of a steep, forested incline. We got into the back of a pickup truck that labored its way up a narrow road that had been bulldozed into the mountainside.

We arrived at the top, a lush plateau, where there were streams and waterfalls, a continuous flowing that never stopped. We sat with our feet in the water and then eventually swam with other visitors. And all the while, the waterfall thundered down from on high, not trying at all, just dropping and plunging and making its noise continuously.

These were the rarest of days here, when the air moved and the brightest of penetrating suns clarified all colors. The water was as blue as it could be, and every green leaf was as green as the depths of refreshing sleep. When the wind blew, it was not hot as it so often was, but cool and refreshing, like the breeze itself was saying, "Look at the colors. Look how bright and clear everything is. Anything is possible."

"I used to come here when I was a child," Rangsei said. "I thought about taking you here when I first met you."

"But you told me your parents didn't want you to date a foreigner when I first asked you out. I had to ask a bunch of times," I said.

"I was lying," she replied, with a tiny smile.

We bought some food and sat by the upper part of the waterfall where placid water drifted by before it cascaded off the edge.

There were ruins everywhere, peeking through the jungle. Some toppled pillars stood here and there by the stream. Hundreds of years before my own country's swampy land was plowed and covered with insecticide, there were those laboring here over strange structures for their own ends, which were now murky, if not lost forever.

People nearby were taking incessant photos of the moldering ruins. We were all surely thinking, "How careless these people were to go to ruin. What we have built will forever stand."

Near us, at the stream's edge, was a dark-skinned shiny man, old as the rocks, who threw out his patched net so he could catch even the smallest fish, as that was all there was to be had. He threw his net out in hopes of the rare bigger fish that were rarer by the day, as more old people dotted the stream, each with their nets, all hoping for the big fish. He had a plastic bucket filled with tiny silver fish, all shivering in anger at their fate.

The old man eyed us suspiciously, as if calculating something, before going back to his task.

"There's gold in the river from the old kingdom," Rangsei explained. "It still washes down from the mountains sometimes—flashes of gold."

This wilderness was once the center of a great empire, but centuries ago, its time was over, its greatness legendary, its names and stories lost, its stones melting under the consuming jungle. Incorruptible gold would leak out, washed down by the waters.

"If the old man can find even the smallest of fragments, he will be rich and count himself lucky," she continued. "But he must be careful and hide it. Rangers patrol the area and will confiscate any gold that the old fisherman finds. Then it disappears. Some rich man gets it."

"I hope the old man finds gold someday," I said.

"I hope he does too," she said.

I thought I had made the right choice coming to this country. Maybe I would end up in a Mercedes being driven to a big mansion. And how odd that I was here now with this girl, so different to me, in this remote place. She was watching me.

"It's a nice place, right?" she asked, playfully.

"Yes, it's beautiful, but I like it because you are here," I said.

She liked this reply.

"Why do you like my country?" she said, probing.

"This is an interesting place. I didn't know much about it before I was transferred here from Bangkok."

I did not have an actual answer. I was a young man and had no idea why I ended up anywhere. My answer to her reduced this place of strange history to nothing. I knew the reason I was here was related to ambition, but I did not say that.

Thunder stuttered in the distance. The air was crystal clear.

"I'm going to live and work here, I think. I do like it." It was not a satisfactory summation of who I was and what I was going to be. Someday, I was sure I would have a better reply. I had worlds to conquer and fortunes to make.

I added, "There's no place like this now." It seemed a better answer. We smiled together.

The wind blew through the trees, awakening the green of rain. Rangsei and I walked downstream from the waterfall to where the water was navigable.

Here, boats could be rented to drift down the stream a bit. We got in a rickety boat that was leaking a little. We drifted along. The water sounded like chimes as it rustled over clumps of rocks here and there.

I saw a vivid silver plane flying overhead, almost out of sight, bypassing this country, my world, threading its exhaust like the foam of beer at an angle dissecting the sky.

I cannot remember what we talked about that day. I'm sure it wasn't weighty. It was the shorthand of the young and vital designed to be together. It was as if she had always been in my life and always would be. As I floated along, I felt as though the hair on my head was floating upward in ecstasy.

Soon, masses of clouds were puffing up into monumental thunderheads. We could hear thunder rumbling, almost like distant artillery, smooth and round sounds by the time they reached us, but certainly sharp where they emanated from.

Our boat made its way down to the next cataract of the stream, where the boats would be collected and towed back upstream. A boatman there pulled our boat in. I wanted to go back upstream and drift back down again. It was a short hike, since the stream twisted from where we got on to where we got off. However, the thunder and the clouds were closer now and there were some black ones boiling up nearby.

Rangsei spoke in the jabbering local language to the boatman there, who was frantically shooing us away from the water, while gesturing at the gathering clouds.

To me, it looked like there would still be plenty of time before the rains arrived, and I thought how wonderful it would be to drift along again, seeing the trickles of water seeping through the cracks of the boat, knowing it would be all right, before finally coming to a meandering stop.

Rangsei refused to go back and take another boat ride, warning, "Be careful. You don't know everything. You have to be careful of the flood."

Maybe I had argued about this too emphatically. I did not realize I was talking so much—like a know-it-all foreigner with my opinions on everything.

Eventually, we became a little cross with each other. We hiked up a trail to get back to the trucks that would take us back down the mountain.

Our path skirted the edge of the stream that led to the waterfall. The previous bright, clear sky was now grey, and, from the ground, a delicate mist was rising. The smell of dampness arose—the smell of fertile soil and rotting decay, budding plants awakened by the rain and fungus gnawing away at the fibers of ancient trees—then a rumbling. I stopped, thinking this was an earthquake, a physical shaking of the land. But from the distance came a slushing sound, and it became louder and more insistent, until it was a roar, right upon us. Rangsei grabbed my hand and then we ran up the side of the hill away from the stream.

A few moments later, a swell of water rushed down, engulfing the stream as well as the trail beside it. This was a flash flood created somewhere far off where the rains fell on mountains and was sieved into valleys which sieved into other valleys, and all of this propelled a larger and larger untamable mass of water to inundate areas far from the rain itself.

I wondered if the people back at the waterfall had been washed away. Had the man at the boat pier fled in time? I thought of the rickety boats and the small dock where we had alighted. Maybe this flooding was a common occurrence, and everyone was ready, and the boats were tied up and the people moved to a safe distance as a matter of course. I did not know, and I could not go back to check because the way was flooded.

"I told you it wasn't safe," she said sweetly. She knew this place better than I did, I guess.

Holding hands, we cut through the forest to where we thought the pickup trucks that had brought us were. For a time, we got lost, finally going up a steep hill that we soon realized could not possibly be the right way. Then suddenly, we were there, tumbling out of the forest into the gravel parking lot where trucks were waiting patiently to take us down the mountain.

5

A week passed, Chiang retreated into the splendor of his life in Thailand, and the events of the party at the prime minister's house faded into a picturesque memory.

I was stationed in the control room as usual, my mind wandering, when Don and John, in a panic, burst in. John had a wire-crimping tool in his hand, and both were wearing plastic gloves, as if in the middle of a technical task. I had never seen them enter my control room before.

"Are they here yet?" John said to me as if I was purposely withholding information. "Inside the compound?"

They both looked at me with wide eyes, and, as they had rarely spoken to me previously, I was surprised. I sat back and took my time with my answer.

John again said, as if giving me an order, "Are they in the building?" But before I could answer, they ran out of the room. I followed them, and when I got to the reception area, they were pacing about, wide-eyed and fearful. Noi was there, completely placid, as if nothing could surprise her.

I looked out of the glass doors toward the front gate of the compound. There, parked outside the gates, was a military armored personnel carrier blocking the entrance. Several soldiers with rifles were standing there, as if they were waiting for orders to enter the compound.

I sensed Don at my side, looking out at the soldiers. "Oh no, this isn't good," he said.

"What's going on?" I asked, trying not to seem too alarmed.

John approached the window too. "It's the contract," he said, then adding, "but maybe more."

"What contract?" I said.

They both looked at me like I was stupid.

"CLB has a 99-year concession on its exclusive rights to this market," Don said.

"You see, it's crazy," John said. "No one gets a 99-year concession. That's colonial-era rules. It's not standard business practice anymore. It's crony capitalism—where the guy in power can carve up the valuable parts of his country and hand them over to a foreign company for generations."

"But not this time," Don said. "The U.N. is still in charge of some things, and they are pressuring the government to disavow the 99-year agreements. It's no issue for Thaw Kai. He'll just sell the rights again and get all the bribes again."

"But for Chiang, he won't accept it. He never loses," John added.

"So, Thaw Kai is blockading the compound to force Chiang to sign a new, shorter contract."

As I soaked up this information, Don and John exited the reception area without another word. Noi had vanished too. Then the power went out. Yeah, Thaw Kai was putting the squeeze on.

I returned to the control room. I wondered if we were out of business now and if I still had a job, if my dreams of glory here were ended. I understood now that this was what Chiang and Thaw Kai had been jousting over at his home—the impending cancellation of the contract with CLB.

The rest of the staff must have been more aware than I was and had already cleared out. I grabbed my briefcase full of papers and then exited the building by a side door.

I thought I would cross over the compound to the largest studio buildings—the ones used for news broadcasting—and exit on the road on that side of the compound. The big bosses would have to sort out their disagreements. I did not want to be part of this mess in the meantime.

As I crossed the compound, a few people scurried about, going in different directions with worried looks on their faces. I got to the studio building and entered by a side door at the backup generator. Once inside, I looked down the long hall that ran the length of the building. There were already military men at the far end, moving along, looking here and there through the doors that led off the hallway.

I backed out of the hallway, exited the same way I came in, and skirted the edge of the building, stumbling over various large cables until I got to the street on the other side of the compound. A crowd of staff was by the gate, but their exit was also being blocked by military men and APCs.

I gave up trying to escape and walked back to the control room. I peeked out the back door at the signal house. Don and John were dropping piles of papers into an oil drum in which a fire was burning joyously. Handfuls of cables were also going in. It smelled bad. Don was tamping it all down with a stick.

Tieng came into the room, crestfallen. "The company's contract was cancelled. We will have to close down," he said dramatically, almost tearfully.

An hour passed and the CLB compound remained sealed. The waiting created alternating periods of agitation and resignation in me. I thought back to what I had witnessed at the Lion's Den between Chiang and Thaw Kai. In a place like this, deploying the military was bureaucratic action, because, for anything to happen, it took bald force. But surely Chiang would save us. He couldn't lose.

With the air conditioning off, the air grew unimaginably hot. I sat in the darkened control room not moving, as I had learned that in these climes, stillness meant coolness and even thinking would cause one to sweat. Better to embody stillness, body and mind.

In the late afternoon, I walked back out to the deserted reception area. I looked out to the front gate where there was now movement and loud talking. The revving sounds of APCs being moved back and forth rattled the glass doors of the building. The unmistakable smell of diesel fumes arose. Military men were waving their arms at other military men who were blocking the entrance to the compound.

One soldier raised his pistol into the air and shook it fervently at the other soldiers. I thought maybe this might be our own friendly military men, allies from the nearby base, attempting to break our siege, but I was too far away to see their insignias. In any case, there clearly was a dispute among those at the blockade.

I got up on top of the reception desk, Noi's desk, and sat there irreverently, cross-legged, as, from this vantage point, I could see the entire scene unfolding. Soldiers yelled and gestured. Dark exhaust smoke from the vehicles wafted up.

CLB workers were wandering about in the courtyard, slowly moving towards the gate, with sad looks on their faces. Eventually, a crowd pushed up to the gates, expecting to be let out. It was quitting time, and nothing could hold them for another second. More and more staff arrived, until it was a large crowd: hungry workers expecting to go home and do their laundry in their little apartments.

Then, a single shot was fired into the air. A bit of blue smoke exited the gun as the bullet flew skyward. The sound was a firecracker yelp that echoed for a moment into the compound.

The crowd of workers froze and the yelling between the military men ceased. I was suddenly tense. It is all fun and games until someone starts shooting.

Then, like a dam bursting, the soldiers gave way and pulled back their vehicles from the entrance. The crowd of workers flowed outwards through the gate and onto the street.

A few people who had cars parked in the compound drove out frantically, forcing others to leap out of the way. A car was a status symbol, and they certainly did not want to get their status symbol locked up under military control. Within minutes, the parking lot in front of the building completely cleared.

Don and John ambled into the reception room. I could tell from their posture that circumstances had changed.

"They made a deal," John said, "Chiang gave up the 99-year concession."

"You're off the hook," Don said, slapping me on the shoulder.

"What do you mean?" I said.

After an instant, I realized they were joking with me about their own fears. Then we all laughed like men who had surmounted great odds—me, John, who was my muscular doppelganger, and Don. They continued out the door and it banged loudly behind them. The soldiers and trucks were pulling away on the street.

This thought appeared in my head—Chiang would have his revenge. It was spoken to me as clearly as if he was saying it out loud. It was a realization from the part of me that was forever scheming. Then I figured I should get out of the building too. I picked up my briefcase, jumped off the desk, and walked towards the front gate to make my escape.

Phong appeared, with his broom, from under the one tree in the compound, mechanically sweeping the grounds as if nothing unusual was happening. His head tilted up to notice me, and then he went back to sweeping. He eyed me with suspicion, as he always did.

Every place takes its turn, I guess. History is a long march to make people become used to the outrageous. Everything that can happen will eventually happen.

Beirut was once an idyllic place, home to retirees who soaked up the pleasant Mediterranean air. Yet, it became a byword for lawlessness—and a failed state.

Acapulco was once idyllic, where resorts catered to the wealthy of North America. Then, violent drug gangs piled up bodies.

I recalled the party and the meeting between Thaw Kai and Chiang. In this land, too many things had happened. Thaw Kai could sit atop its mountain and kick back at Chiang, who deigned to outmaneuver him. One owned the country; the other could buy it. There had to be something for me here. I was pretty confident I had this under control.

6

Pallets of satellite dishes and crates were arriving by the day, despite the cancellation of CLB's concession. The business of the network continued on as usual, and the events of the blockade of the compound seemed to have been forgotten.

Mike came in and asked me where Don and John were.

"Always in there," I said, gesturing towards the signal house outside. He exited out the back door to the signal house.

He then returned and paced through the control room several times, becoming more agitated.

"Where are they?" he said to himself, before leaving again.

I wondered what role Mike really played. I probably could have found out more from Noi, but I did not want to play her game by asking her to gossip.

Tieng, who I gradually learned knew everything that was going on, told me Mike was a rapper.

"Is that so?" I said, deciding not to argue with him about it. It may have been an assumption based on Mike being a big, cool-looking, black guy. Tieng added that Mike gambled with the locals and knew everyone.

I guessed that Mike was one of those people who knew what was happening with the rank and file on the street as well as with the top bosses. Maybe something about his otherness. The locals and their hierarchies did not know where he should be, and he could move between them, seeing all.

Mike reentered the control room. "You haven't seen them?" he asked.

"No."

He looked at his watch—time was ticking away on something. Then he looked at me as if he were making a decision.

He finally said, "Hey, you want to give me a hand? I've got to pick something up at the airport." Then, to himself, "This is actually better. No locals or the firm."

"What's this about?" I said.

"Just give me a hand. It's no big deal. It'll just take a few minutes. Something from Chiang."

He said it as if he knew it would entice me and my ambitions.

I followed Mike outside to a short flatbed truck with a winch on the back. As Mike pulled out onto the hot bright street, he said, to no one in particular, "This is the place to be." Then, seeing me squint at the afternoon sun, he handed me a pair of sunglasses. He put on sunglasses as well, as we rumbled along.

"Thaw Kai has quite a place," I said. "Why didn't you go?"

"You know, he has his own jail out there," Mike said, ignoring my question.

"Fun to be able to do whatever you want, I guess," I replied.

"He can put people right in it and let them out when he pleases. That's power," he said, finishing the thought somewhat ruefully.

"What is it we are picking up?" I said in a flat tone, as if the pretense of initial conversation was now dispensed with.

"It's something special from Chiang," he said conspiratorially. "Nobody crosses him and gets away with it. As you probably guessed, there are quite a bit more... uses to the place we're working at other than broadcasting the news and noodle commercials."

After another pause, where it seemed he was weighing how much to divulge, he said, "It's special communications equipment. That's all. You'll see soon." And then, in the first flash of seriousness, Mike turned to me and said, "Be sure not to say anything about this. Not to anybody."

"I won't," I said.

"It's important," he said.

"I won't say anything," I replied.

"Don't mention this even to John or Don."

"I won't," I said. I was elated. Now we were getting somewhere. Something big was happening, and I was a part of it.

"That guy Phong," I said. "He sweeps the grounds at CLB, and I also saw him in uniform at the base."

"He's sort of a mascot. He's harmless," Mike said. "But don't trust anyone," he added. "Even me." He smiled his typical smile.

Then there was a sudden silence—a pause in the universe. Mike leaned forward towards the steering wheel, hunching up as if resisting something.

"I was not there at Thaw Kai's. Too conspicuous, they said." It was this that bit at him. "I should have been there. I... It's always something like this. It is not just being black here, it's everything. Being big. I like it, I should love it, but... if I'm not vigilant, I will always be seen as the smiling hulk in any room. That's what everyone thinks, right?"

"Yeah, well some, I suppose." I had to admit it and I was not sure I wanted to argue the point.

"It's not that exactly, it's what it means. How many times have you been arrested? In handcuffs?"

"Never." I smiled slightly in amusement.

"See, a white boy laughs at that. Every place I go, I am in handcuffs. Police in Thailand once stopped me in a taxi, said I was hiding my face as I went by. I was only looking at a map. They would never stop you for that."

I spoke without thinking and without hesitation, "I know."

"They are mainly good out here—better than in the States—but I am still this, this... thing. You are too, a white boy in Asia, but it is not the same. You can skip between the raindrops... can do anything, I should be able to do anything... like you coming out here, doing what you want. But you don't know what it is like to be seen how they see me."

The truck hurtled forward, raising dust from the road behind it.

"Conspicuous!" he continued. "And they smiled as they said it. I know what it means, and they don't even know it's racist. I'm just something to them. Just a..." and his words escaped in real bitterness, "black giant." I could see behind his words, a thick bile. "This has happened to me my whole life."

"Yeah, I can imagine," I said. There wasn't much more to say.

Seconds passed. Then it was as if the mood broke unexpectedly, and Mike was assessing why he had told me this. He leaned back in his seat, and we were two Westerners wearing sunglasses like the Blues Brothers again.

"Hmmm," Mike grinned ruefully. "Got me to talk. Nice job."

I said nothing. Better he think I was as canny as he thought I was.

"Are Don and John on Chiang's side?" I asked.

"They are on both sides. And on top of that, they aren't even here," he said, laughing.

We drove along on the far edge of the airport. Hangers and cargo sheds lined the road. Each had its own exit to the service road that surrounded the airport.

Mike turned into one of these sectioned-off areas with a large hanger. Sitting before the closed doors of the hanger were two pallets of boxes, wrapped in plastic, like they had been placed outside in anticipation of them being picked up. Otherwise, the place was deserted. We jumped out and Mike examined the labels on the pallets, looked up at me and nodded. The winch on the truck was not working, and we had to wrestle the pallets onto the truck by sliding them on long boards.

The moment they were on, we stopped to take a breath. Mission accomplished. Then, in the distance, coming towards us was a line of what looked like military trucks, careening along the road that circled the airport.

"I don't think they're our guys," Mike said, referring to our friendly troops from the city base—the place where Chiang had given his speech. We jumped back into the truck and Mike started driving the opposite way from them, still on the road that tightly hugged the borders of the airport. It did seem as though the military trucks were pursuing us now.

Mike turned onto a dirt road that went through a wooded area. We were still quite a bit ahead of our pursuers. Along the road were mounds of garbage—clearly a dumping area for waste from the airport. Mike stopped the truck and pushed the pallets off the truck next to one of the piles of garbage. They came down with a thud.

"Stay here. I'll be back," he said.

Without a chance for me to protest, he jumped back in the truck and drove off, leaving me standing with the two pallets next to the piles of trash. The pile was made up of all manner of things—bags of fast-food packaging, other pallets and packing material, and even a mattress. The two pallets in their plastic wrap from Chiang blended in with the clutter of the other garbage. I heard vehicles approaching and ran back and hid behind a tree with my heart pounding as the pursuing military trucks roared past. I watched them pass the pallets, sitting there in plain sight.

Then it was quiet. It was bracingly scary. People were after me. I was alone here, far, far away in a godforsaken place, a remote backwater, even for the Thais. But I never accepted fate. I could see fate coming and would strike it, breaking it apart as I denied it. Later in my life, as an old man, fate would lie on top of me like an illness and thoughts of bursting through its trials would vanish. But at the time, I was a hale man, unencumbered by my own history, and I would stride forward while others cowered.

Another flatbed truck drove up—a military one. The driver spotted me and slammed on the brakes. He jumped out and he ran over to me.

He was skinny as a rail and probably in his 20s or 30s. I could not tell the ages of anyone here, as most men looked both young and old. He pushed his thumb under the collar of his uniform to show me the white unit pin he wore, indicating he was from a friendly base. One of us.

We were both much smaller than Mike and I wondered how we were going to get the pallets up on the truck, as this one had no winch at all. Despite the soldier's skinniness, he was all strength, and we both pushed and willed those pallets up on the truck using all our adrenaline-driven strength, then we jumped in and sped off, fearful the unfriendly military trucks would return at any moment.

7

Police here would customarily stop vehicles plying the roads, especially commercial ones, inspect their occupants, and find an infraction to extract a bribe over. This would happen at checkpoints created by a long board swung down to stop traffic, counterbalanced on the other end by a concrete block.

We approached such a checkpoint, the gate still in place as we rolled up. An old portly police officer stood there, slouched, looking sleepy. When we stopped, however, a soldier jumped out from a clump of foliage with his gun drawn. He gestured us out of the vehicle.

As we exited, I could see that the unit pin on his collar was brown—not one of our friendly city base soldiers. He looked at both of us, and then at me a second time. Then, with a smirk, he jumped into the cab of the truck and sped off. The sleepy cop raised the barrier for him just in time.

The white-pinned soldier with me said something in the local language to me, then placed his hands on his face as if he were about to scream. I imagined he would be in trouble for losing Chiang's cargo. He ran down a small embankment by the road towards some shophouses on the adjacent street. Raising the alarm, I thought. The sleepy policeman at the checkpoint gave me a look as if to say, "It's got nothing to do with me!"

At the side of the road was a battered motorcycle, the policeman's motorcycle, no doubt. I looked at it and then at the truck with the pallets from Chiang receding in the distance.

I walked to the motorcycle, keeping one eye on the policeman. The keys were in it. Time to make a decision, I thought. It would not look too good if I lost the shipment. It was my chance to be noticed. I thought of Andrew back in Bangkok and his slow march to death, working at the school.

I jumped on the motorcycle and sped off down the road. The policeman only slowly lifted one arm as I sped away, perhaps a protest for taking his bike, perhaps waving goodbye. I did not know. I watched him as I rode away to make sure he was not going to shoot me in the back. That happened often here.

I was now sputtering along on a motorcycle with no helmet and at twilight. Then it started to rain.

After five minutes of empty roads, sometimes thinking I had lost the truck, I came upon it. It was there in the rain, and the soldier was standing outside the cab, regarding a waterlogged part of the road with trees all around. The road looked impassible, as a torrent of water was crossing it and falling into a steep-sided canal along the side of the road. I coasted up almost silently as the intensity of the rain fortuitously increased. We were alone on this road now. I walked towards him. He turned to me and made no further movement, standing his ground.

I could not go around him, only through him, so I did, rushing up and trying to push him aside in my efforts to get to the truck. I had foolishly thought fighting was like in the movies—punching, but soon we were grappling like wrestlers for some indeterminate time, neither being able to turn the other. I was surprised at how his small frame could hold its position so firmly. I suddenly wondered if he would pull out a gun and shoot me. He did not appear to have one, but in my hubris, I did not think to look before I began fighting. What about a knife? Every good soldier should have one. I was now experiencing the dread fear of injury and I wished for escape. It is a terror that only one who has fought for his life knows— a gladiator, a knight, a cad in a foreign land.

We stood upright for a moment, still gripping arm to hand and hand to arm, and then tottered as we tumbled down the mud bank into the canal. Trees on the other side of the canal were blurry sticks in the rain and the water was black and foul, as it was in all of these waterways.

He got me in the stomach, either with a punch or a kick, catching me on an exhale, completely expelling the breath from my body. It took all my concentration to continue to remain upright as I gasped for air and attempted to resume the pattern of breathing.

We both scrambled in the muck at the water's edge. Then we let go of each other as if to take a break. The soldier was half in the water, nearly up to his waist and both of my legs were stuck in the mud. I tried to pull myself out without losing my shoes. The rain was coming down in thick sheets now. The soldier looked up at me, somehow both defiant and expressionless. It was the moment in any fight where both parties peer out of their adrenaline and anger and say to themselves, "This is really happening."

He lunged at me with his steely grip, and I could not disengage. I had to win this. I decided what to do. I leaned forward and held him under, my own mouth and nose just managing to stay above the thick water. It did not take long. I then wondered why I had done it.

His grasp relaxed and I left him there. I crawled out of the water, caked with black clay. I cursorily brushed off my shirt, almost chuckling at the ridiculousness of brushing the mud away. I was trembling, and my hands were covered with mud.

I scrambled up from the ditch. I felt for my wallet, thinking it might be floating in the water, a tell-tale sign of my guilt, but it was still safely in my pocket. The rain fell like static across a TV screen, obscuring the landscape. No witness. The road was serendipitously empty and still. All of nature's eyes turned away and I began to think I would be the only one who would ever know what had happened. The luck of the white man in a foreign land. Mike had said it. I started to think I could get away with it. Even the rain was conspiring to wash away my tracks.

A convoy of vehicles emerged out of a white sheet of water, shocking me. Men were already emerging from them before I could think of what to do.

It was Amnuay and men from our friendly military base. Still, I imagined that I was being arrested.

Amnuay walked directly to me and smiled, a smile of his mouth only. His eyes were saying something like, "You did not fill out the proper paperwork." However, he said, "Good job." His face hardened into a look of satisfaction, and he gestured to the soldiers to check the pallets. I wondered what the top company man was doing here, but I realized that the cargo—which I soon learned was special radios—was important enough for Amnuay himself to retrieve.

Then, it all went oddly slowly, as if there was no urgency at all. Soldiers carefully checked the pallets. They were more interested in the condition of the pallets than the body floating in the water. The tattooed face of Chiang's Gurkha bodyguard emerged from one of the vehicles. He carefully inspected the scene, then nodded at me in admiration, like we were fellow warriors.

Other men walked back and forth in the area, perhaps looking for any clues that might have been left. I watched attentively as if I were attending a funeral. Then the dead man was fished from the canal. Not a bit of blood. They wedged him in behind the truck's seats. I saw that his gun was in a holster on the seat of the truck. He could have run back and picked it up and killed me. He should have, in fact.

It made me feel faint, but I resisted this. I was not going to appear like a fool in front of all these men. Then I had an even stronger feeling—that I was going to vomit. It felt like I was being shaken from above by the hair, my body beginning to waver out of this world for a time. But I still resisted. Yes, this feeling was the world, the universe, my schoolteachers from long ago, everything that had tried to civilize me—it was trying to force me to know something. It said I could not get away with this and I would collapse. But I resisted. I would not feel bad. Time to be a tough guy. It was already done. I spat into a puddle there in the rain. I spat in the face of the universe.

They turned the truck around. Amnuay directed me into a military truck. Another man picked up the motorcycle.

I said to Amnuay, "I stole it from a policeman." It seemed an absurd thing to say at that point, but then Amnuay would be just the person to tie up this loose end.

Amnuay just said, "Okay," and a soldier, first looking at the license plate, rode off on the motorcycle. I did not care, and I never heard anything more about it.

I got in the truck with Amnuay. The air-conditioning was on, and it made my nose run, but it was nice to be in a controlled environment again. The Gurkha got in the driver's seat, and we drove off.

The Gurkha leaned back toward me from the front seat and warned me, "Don't go out tonight."

"Why?" I said.

"Tonight, the spirit of the man you killed will be roaming." He said this with complete seriousness, as if it was the most important of advice from warrior to warrior.

"I won't," I replied.

They dropped me at my apartment without me giving any directions, apparently knowing right where it was.

I threw away my shoes, thinking that if I had left footprints, in spite of the rain, they might be traced back to me.

I had read the words of guilt by Dostoyevsky. His words were punishing. I suppose, like all men, when I was awakened at 3:00 am by the tail end of a dream I could not remember, I could feel something bad was out there waiting for me and that I was guilty of something. This was not the ambition I was searching for. It was not the adventure I had imagined.

I walked out to the porch and looked out. It was a moonless night, but the sky was pinkish and bright from the streetlights. In the distance, in a perfectly straight line, rain was coming. From one end of the horizon to the other, it came. The rushing air was churning up a cloud of dust. Like the foam of an advancing wave, it swept forward, and behind it was a towering wall of clouds, at once boiling and sleek, like bubbling milk cascading over and through the dirty shophouses.

It was too early for things to happen. Or maybe there are some things that can only happen at this time. Half asleep, my anticipation rose. I began to think I should flee, but I wanted to see what was to come. I did not believe in karma but could not help feeling I would have to pay one way or another for this thrill.

When I was a young boy, our teacher took my class to a meatpacking plant, ostensibly for us to understand the modern industries of our country. However, she was actually trying to create in us the urge to be noble vegetarians. We were shown the slabs of meat and the cutting of the meat and the viscera and offal on the cement floor. It was pink and vivid, and, in a way, sickening, but being the boy I was, it made me hungry, and I said this, much to the laughter of the students and to the teacher's chagrin.

Now, as I saw my own victim in my mind's eye, I almost wished that there had been some of that pink viscera—or that I had shot or stabbed him and there was thus some evidence of the horror. The horror of what I had done. Something marked in red.

He was there, but not alive anymore, not even a tiny spot of blood congealing in the sun to let the world know what had happened.

PART IV

1

Even after what had happened, the world continued. I awoke the next morning and went back to work, for a time concerned that something had changed forever. But things were the same. No one took any notice. It was almost a disappointment.

Then, a military man arrived in the control room to inform me I was summoned to our friendly military base that evening. It sounded like an order.

I immediately found Mike and asked him what was going on. Might it be safer for Chiang's cause for me to go missing in this country of so many dangers? Better to remove a potential wild card who no one really knew and who had now served his purpose. They could say I overdosed and never woke up, or better yet, wrecked out drunk on a motorbike in the rain, drowned in a canal. It was not uncommon to see motorcyclists dead on the roads. They were as common as the weather.

By the time my grieving relatives arrived, I would have already been cremated. How awful to be converted to photos in rarely seen photo albums. And if my name were not written on the back of the photos, the next generation could only say, "Who was that?"

But no, Mike said it was fine. "You proved your worth, kid," he said. "There's no need to bring that up again. What had to happen, happened."

"Don and John..." I began.

"They are not involved. Never involved. All the stuff you've seen. It doesn't exist... and you don't exist to them."

I realized that the dispute between Thaw Kai and Chiang might be seen by greater powers, such as nations, as advantageous to their goals, and that little people like me, carrying out our little schemes, could be playing into some larger plans.

As if reading my mind, Mike answered, "Don't worry. We are doing our own thing here. This is all a local matter. Tonight, we are going to a very private party. We're going to discuss something. I'll be there this time."

"Discuss what?"

Mike put his fingers to his lips to signal silence.

"It'll be worth your time."

So that was that. I had wanted in on something and here it was.

Later that day, Noi found me. She was annoyed that the military man had refused to allow her to relay the message to me.

"He just walked right in," she complained to me. Then, perhaps aware she was allowing me to realize her annoyance, said, "What are you getting mixed up in with these army men?"

She said, "army men" like she was saying "mafia." It probably was not far from the truth.

"It's just a gathering, a party, I think."

"Don't jeopardize your working documents over anything dodgy." She said it in a strange way, like she was implying she had some control over my employment.

But by this time, I knew I had an in with Mike, Amnuay, and now Chiang. There was nothing she could do. I smiled, maybe even smirked, back at her. I was feeling pretty confident.

That evening, an army van drove me over to the base. I was dropped off at the six-story building, the one where Chiang had given his speech. The bottom floors were dark now, but light and music issued from the upper floors. Okay, a real gathering was going on. I was not going to be disposed of.

My own apartment building was five stories tall, but it only had stairs. I lived on the third floor and wearied of plodding up and down. But this building, fantastically enough, had an elevator in it, a rarity here.

Mike was there, in the semi-darkness, by the elevator, apparently waiting for me.

A party was being held, Mike explained as we rode up in the lift. It was to commemorate the anniversary of a political party involved in funding the military base.

The lift doors opened onto the gathering. It was all military men standing about, but not the lean ones who did all the work. These were all the older, fatter men. They were the types who gave orders and hiked up their pants over their waists, to be belted at the stomach.

The men all went silent and stared at us as we exited the lift. A military man, I think an M.P., ushered us through to a section of darkened rooms. It was another meeting area with chairs and tables stacked up in one corner. The glow from the city was the only light and it fell across the space sharply, alternating between darkness and a clear grey.

Amnuay sat at a table, alone, puffing seriously on a cigarette. He looked at both of us, then at Mike, and waved him away. The M.P. led Mike out. I did not see Mike's reaction to this.

Amnuay directed me to sit.

A few steps behind him in the shadows, I noticed the Gurkha standing, as if ready to spring into action. It was a dramatic tableau that emphasized the gravity of this situation.

Amnuay was distracted, not looking at me. "You remember Ganju," Amnuay said, gesturing over his shoulder to the Gurkha guard. I nodded, although I had never heard his name before. Although in shadow, Ganju's tattooed face was strangely sharp in the dark. Ganju, Mike, and I—we were all conspicuous in our own ways.

Amnuay continued looking away from me out the window, as if he was pondering something disturbing.

"As you surely realize, the situation with the government has become bad. It's not fair. It's not democratic." He said this with almost a mock sadness, like someone who did not know nor care what democracy was. He then sighed in resignation.

"We have to make a change. Do you understand?" he said, turning to me.

I was supposed to understand and was not sure I did, but I did not want him to know that. I said, "Yes." Might as well say yes.

"We will need your support in some of the technical aspects."

I was starting to understand—the conflict with Thaw Kai, the pallets of radios, and the man who never loses.

"I understand," I said. Then I added, "But what about the 99-year concession? What about the United Nations?"

"Fuck the United Nations," Amnuay said. He said this as if he were not used to making strong proclamations in this foreign tongue of English. His English was restricted to the communication of sentences carefully constructed to be grammatically correct. His face turned to me as if wanting to see how I would react to his temerity.

"Okay," I said. "Yes," I added, perhaps uncertainly.

He paused, as if weighing what I said, then tapped the ash off his cigarette. He then put out his hand to me and we shook hands, properly up and down and firmly. I felt it meant that we were agreeing to something.

It was an unexpectedly brief meeting, and I soon found that it was because someone was waiting for me. Amnuay stood, directing me to come with him. Ganju led the way as we climbed a further flight of stairs from the fifth to the sixth floor. This extra floor was clearly an additional floor added after the main building and its lift was completed, probably ordered to be built by a general to whom no one would dare ask if the structure was strong enough to support the further weight.

This higher floor was another open area for gatherings and had a dramatic row of large windows that opened the room to the west and the dusty city spread out below. Stacks of chairs for events were everywhere here, along with utilitarian red carpeting and an elevated platform for a speaker, hidden in the blackness. The lights were off here as well, and the dim city light poured in through the windows to give the room a murky redness.

Then I saw him. Chiang was there, standing in the darkness, the secrecy of the moment implicit in this tableau. I had not realized he was in the country again. His back was to me as he looked out over the town at night.

Amnuay, being the diplomat, extended his hand to direct me toward Chiang, as if I might wander off in another direction. Ganju stood back, ever watchful.

"All is forgiven," Chiang said looking at me sincerely with his head tilted a bit. It seemed to me he was saying it was okay that I had killed the soldier. He was a soldier after all. This was war. I think I was grasping for such a sentiment, as the event was something I could never tell to anyone. It made what he said a salve to me.

"Amnuay has briefed you?"

"Yes," I said. I felt like saying, "Sort of."

Chiang continued. "Please understand we are forced to do this. It's so unfair."

This sounded very much like what a person would say before committing violence. Still, I was intrigued.

"This is going to restore fairness and peace." He emphasized "is" as if he thought my Western sensibilities might be doubting him. "It is going to be an improvement. Restore democracy."

Amnuay added, "We will need you for some of the logistics."

Chiang paused dramatically. He looked out at the rows of buildings spread out in a random geometry below. People were sleeping out there, the poor and the rich, and we were at this high place, planning something.

"So, Bert, can we count on you?" Chiang said graciously. I don't think he had said my name before, and hearing it made me realize I was here, and this was being asked of me.

From this high place, only occasional harsh white points of light illuminated shops or cafes below. The city was yet to be infested with the orangish streetlights that made every modern city glow with perpetual dusk even at midnight.

I looked at the city stretched out below me and then back to the tycoon Chiang. I wanted to be involved in something, and this was surely something. Could I go on just working week after week without risking something in this far place?

"Yes," I said.

Chiang tilted his head slightly, and in the most subtle of voices, said, "Thank you." He looked relieved.

"I noticed a secure communications room at Thaw Kai's office," I said. Chiang and Amnuay exchanged glances as if this proved I was the right person.

And then, as if a floodgate had opened and Chiang could address me frankly, he said, "We will catch him at the Lion's Den. He will not get away with this."

Then he looked directly at me and smiled in the way Thai men did sometime, sincerely and maniacally, completely justified in what he was intending. It was the type of expression that made me happy I was on his side. I could read between the lines—he was going to overthrow the government.

"Once the changeover is complete, I would like the concession for the government preparatory schools," I said, staking my claim. I knew it was a monopoly and very profitable.

Chiang and Amnuay exchanged glances as if calculating. Amnuay then nodded back at Chiang.

He thought for a moment.

"That is your background, right?" Chiang said.

"Yes," I replied.

"When this is done," he said, "Yes, we can do that."

It seemed as though he were really saying, "If this could be done." It made me wonder at the enormity of what we were doing.

Chiang then said, "I'm happy you are with us. Amnuay will coordinate with you. As this is a very serious matter, so there will be a consideration for your participation," Amnuay said.

"I understand," I said, and then, "Thank you."

This wrapped up what they wanted to tell me. I *waied* them both, and retreated from the darkened room, leaving Chiang standing silently, looking out over the city. I had made my decision. It made me think that a series of collaborators were being brought up to this high place to affirm they would be involved in this scheme.

Did it matter which corrupt despot ran this government? The money would flow. I could be on any side or no side, but this side would be my side. There was no guarantee I would get what I asked for, but it was something more than I had had before.

I returned down the stairs, careful to move past the generals and their party quickly so as not to make them notice me and go silent again. I later learned that this party was the planning event for what was to come, with top men from various cliques coming together to pledge their loyalty to the actions that needed to be taken.

I took the lift back down to the ground floor. My mind was spinning. I was committed. This was real.

I wondered about the "consideration" mentioned. A payment? In the moment, I did not want to be crass by asking about it, but realized I would be taking a big risk, and surely I should have asked, maybe negotiated with them. But in a few days, I would receive a pay-in notice by courier that one million baht (or 25,000 U.S. dollars at the going rate then) had been deposited into my account back in Thailand. It came from a holding company in Singapore that I had never heard of. They were serious about my involvement. Maybe it really was not a lot for what I was risking, but it was a colossal sum to me at the time and it felt good that I was doing something serious.

When I exited the building after my meeting with Chiang that night, I found that Mike and the van were already gone. I breathed deeply in the muggy night air. One gate to the street was open. I walked across the courtyard to it.

As I passed the gate, I heard someone within the gatehouse being savagely beaten. A man's voice cried out in pain a few times and then there was a gentle weeping as another voice berated him. It must have been some military discipline or maybe a private jail, where these factions gained intelligence and traded prisoners with other factions.

I pondered whether it had been planned for me to hear the beating, to drive home how serious my loyalty was to the plan. Then again, this place had a history of brutality. Maybe there was no need for artifice to teach a tiny person like me how dangerous the world could be. Maybe it was just an everyday beating. The only thing better than power was the misuse of it.

2

New fortunes were nearing, and I was elated. I walked back to my apartment, passing between shops and apartments with their laundry hanging like war flags. It was dark, but there were people out, each on their own mission, and I skirted the many food carts that desired to bar my way. I crossed street to street down the narrow alleys, past the plain children and the old men sitting on broken chairs. I pretended that I was being followed. I dodged the dripping water that always fell from some careless eave above. I wanted to continue the thrill of the day and feel that the pressure was on.

Why am I telling you this? No one ever made me sign anything to keep it a secret. Why would I do this? I said yes and it led to a million things. Beyond that, I have never been able to figure it out.

I got to my apartment building. No one was in the lobby, and I saw no one as I trudged up to the third floor. It was the perfect refuge in an otherwise cluttered city.

Rangsei was waiting in the hallway in front of my door. We had made no plans, but she was there, and we were both happy to be together.

She had brought some of the tasty local food in small bags, purchased from the vendors who were everywhere. In my room, she poured them into little bowls arranged on a low table on the floor. We sat on the floor across from each other and shared the meal.

I was more silent than usual, and she noticed this. She reached for the chain around my neck, drawing out the red amulet. She said she would take me to a fortune teller and determine what our future would be.

We finished the meal and slept that night, side by side, when I carried away by a dream. The dream was of a man whose wife died because of something he was responsible for. The wife was a person like me, of my same race and nationality, a person I had forsworn, would never meet, as I was here in uncharted lands. It left me isolated and looking out of the portholes of my own eyes.

I awoke. The doorknob to my room was jiggling. It was a clear sound. I listened. It was there, someone turning the doorknob.

Rangsei remained asleep, gone for now, so I drew myself up, and got quietly out of bed and tiptoed to the door. I peeked out the peephole. I did not see anyone. I put my hand on the doorknob and turned it and cautiously opened the door and looked both ways. No one was there. The hallway was short enough, though, so that someone could have already fled out of sight. They might be there, right around the corner. I could not know for sure. I closed the door, locked it, and set a chair up against the doorknob. Rangsei was peacefully asleep. I was protecting her now.

A few days prior, Rangsei and I had gone to the tourist backpacker area in town and rented bicycles to ride. I thought it would be fun. Rangsei had laughed to herself as we peddled along.

She explained: "If you ride a bicycle, it is a sign that you were too poor to afford a motorcycle. Or you are a rich foreigner with spare time to be out in the sun. It's like deciding to work in the rice fields or pour concrete just for fun."

"I am getting some thumbs up from people as we ride by," I said.

"They think you are insane," she said, chuckling slightly.

She was not afraid to laugh at me. It was comfortable to be together.

The thought of her was getting to me. Where before, as a young man, it was all about sensual agitation, now I could see something different in her, her old face and some future continuity we could have.

I thought of becoming a rich man like Chiang and living in a mansion with Rangsei—impressing her. It made me wonder about a house and a family.

What would it be like to make such an attachment, a dire attachment, in such a land? Loving deeply and then being in this world with so many things that could keep us apart. Could I bear to leave one day, or would I never want to?

I looked at her sleeping and I knew I was made for this. Maybe it was just my lustfulness mixed with love in a soup of thrilling endorphins.

At some point, I fell asleep. Then, a leaf scraping across the oily cement, the whoosh and rumble of sleepless car drivers, a dream or an animal moving, awoke me again. Summoned back, I checked the clock and checked the night sounds. All in order. All in hapless check. I put my arm around her.

3

Every CLB staff member was to wear an ID badge. Security was becoming strict. Noi handed out the identity badges. She announced each of our names as she stood in the door of the control room, summoning us, and each person dutifully went over to her where she handed out the badges.

Without getting up, I told her to set my ID on the table by the door. She walked over to me and placed the ID lanyard around my neck, as if she were knighting me. And she did it with a big sincere smile that made me feel, in spite of myself, that I was being childish in not coming over to her. Some people have that power.

Entry to my control room was now restricted to a few. It was probably something that should have been done anyway for a broadcasting facility. It now permitted my place of work, my control room, to be sectioned off for the secret preparation of communications equipment, and, as I would soon learn, storage for lots of money.

The pallets from the airport chase were brought in. These contained the secure radio equipment as well as a few special "untappable" telephones Chiang had sent.

Tieng was clearly familiar with the equipment as we unpacked it. I asked him if he had worked with this equipment before. He only nodded.

I suspected he had been ordered to watch me carefully. Sometimes he would probe, asking what I "really thought" about what we were doing.

I always expressed enthusiasm to him about our plans but wondered at myself as well. I knew something was happening to me. It was easy to feel privileged. One skirts the laws that everyday people must adhere to—drives a little faster, foregoes the paperwork, confounds the "insolence of office," while, as every man does, accounting oneself reasonable and believing that such indulgences are only for the occasional, entirely appropriate convenience.

My own advanced nation had its symbols and songs that tried to make me care about it. But its demands, applying rules equally to all, now seemed positively dictatorial. In this far-off land, rules that fell according to one's own ability to thwart them started to appear more individualistic and democratic.

Maybe my bold enthusiasm was why I was not already dead. I did not worry too much about anything right then. There would be plenty of time for that later.

The secure equipment we were unpacking would prevent eavesdropping or phone tapping. This was the key for our plans—secure communications ensured that rival military factions, as well as anyone from the international community who cared, would not know what we were doing.

Some of the equipment had been provided by the U.S. as gifts to consequential officials of foreign governments, mainly in developing countries, as a sign of friendship. Other equipment came from China, and I wondered which was more secure.

I began to understand now why all the new security was in place. For several days in a row, bags stuffed with U.S. dollars, Thai baht, and the local currency arrived. The bags were piled behind a row of technical consoles that were set out from the wall so one could get in back to run cables. Soon, the pile reached high enough that one could see them from behind the chest-high consoles. I began to understand the lubricant of revolution. It was money. A lot was required to spread around to make sure that everything went to plan. Bags and bags of it arrived. Oh boy, I should have asked for more money.

Don and John kept to themselves and never came through the tech building again, instead walking around the outside of our building to get to the signal house. It seemed they were not to be part of Chiang's revenge. This was logical, as they were apparently part of something else. But they had to know about all this for sure and that must mean that my own country approved. I could never imagine all the facets of consideration that went into the decision to upend a government. I guess my country had done it many times before and this would not be the last time they looked the other way when someone else took the risk for them.

Ganju was stationed in the room to guard the money. Formerly, I only saw Ganju with his fierce tattooed face, but in the room, day after day, his face and posture relaxed as he sat on a metal folding chair. I started to see the round, ruddy baby face through his tattoos.

He sometimes spoke to Tieng and me. He told us of the knife which he kept at his belt. If it was ever withdrawn, it could not be returned to its sheath without the drawing of human blood. As it was not always practical to stab someone if the blade had to be drawn, the mindful Gurkha would instead make a small slit on his arm, drawing his own blood and thus being able to return the thirsty dagger to its sheath. He proudly showed us the cuts on his arm from this ritual over the years.

Tieng said, "That must have hurt." This was the epitome of Tieng's Thainess, the disdain for human conflict, and the shying away from discomfort.

"Yes, it hurts every time," Ganju said proudly. "I already know doom. It sits on my head smiling." It sounded like a good saying to fortify men. There was little room in modern times for the warrior and brute force, much less a triumphant victory of arms.

I was feeling brotherhood with Tieng and Ganju and thought that both would be good soldiers to go into battle with.

Once, when Ganju left the room for a break, Tieng told me that Ganju held a cyanide capsule in his mouth which he could bite down on to commit suicide in dire circumstances. It seemed about right, Ganju's moon face and its tattoos obscuring who he was and the things he had seen.

Ganju would invariably return from his breaks with a pack of tiny moist sweet cakes that he bought at the streetside. He would then hand them out to all of us and we would all eat them and Ganju would smile as he ate, like a mischievous child.

Mike checked in from time to time. He warned me not to leave town and only go to and from my apartment within the city. I asked him why and he said, "This is our friendly military zone. The boundaries of its influence are here in the center of the city. Other military bases work for other politicians. It's likely, even if they don't know about you specifically, they have some suspicions. These folks are pretty open in the way they talk. So just being part of the CLB and being such," and he paused knowingly, "a conspicuous foreigner here would mean that Thaw Kai's men might be curious."

The plan for the coup was two-fold: first, capture the prime minister in his compound to take over official communications, and then take over the nation's two international airports.

My mission was to secure the radio room where Thaw Kai communicated with military forces, ministries, and mass media around the country.

The radio equipment Chiang had sent and that I had secured at such a great price would ensure secure channels of communication and enable a column of troops to march to the Lion's Den while disguising their movements and intentions.

Once there, Thaw Kai's control of troops could be disabled from the array behind the house, but it was likely that the ultimate control lay here, right within Thaw Kai's home. Once found, a new voice could be broadcast, proclaiming the new government, and ordering Thaw Kai's military cliques to stay in their barracks while control was solidified, along with the insistence that all was calm, life would go on as normal, and there was nothing to see.

The countdown days in the control room passed by. Amnuay would regularly visit and inspect the bags of money, monitoring their slow dispersal. The bags were a timer, and they grew fewer, carried off one by one.

Going to and from work, I began noticing just how many billboards there were extolling Thaw Kai and his party.

I began to buy a couple bottles of beer on the way home to drink in my apartment. It tasted refreshing, and I anticipated the taste. I never drank in front of Rangsei for some reason. "I'm not nursing an addiction. I'm too smart for that," I thought to myself, feeling the pernicious pull and comfort of alcohol in these stressful days.

I organized lists of what we would need and Amnuay advised on the number of men needed to secure the Lion's Den. I was doing something scary and amazing.

In the evening, Ganju traded off his guard duties with a bored-looking Thai man who sat outside the control room, also one of Chiang's personal guards, I think. He refused to speak to anyone.

I could see Noi was barred from our room, but she was a company girl through and through and retreated to her duties at the front desk.

When I first started to work at the school back in Bangkok, there were no encyclopedias searchable in a digital form on computer. The boss wanted the Britannica Encyclopedia digitized so he could search it on his computer. So, he bought a full set and then had teams of workers sit all day, scanning the pages into the computer.

This was the early era of OCR—optical character recognition—and the resulting scanned text had about one out of 10 letters mis-scanned. My job was to read through all the scanned text, fixing one out of every ten mis-scanned letters so it would be correct.

I relished learning new words. One such word was "freebooting." This referred to Americans in the early nineteenth century who went down to Mexico or Nicaragua on a lark to try to overthrow the government, just for the thrill of it.

That word had stuck in my mind and was firing my imagination now. I wondered at the audacity of those young men of an earlier time, so devoid of the propriety of my own age. And now, I was going to freeboot.

4

During our planning, the need for magic increased. Monks were flown in from Thailand to bless the control room and its staff, including me. This was to ensure luck in our undertaking.

Meanwhile, Rangsei had been asking me to go to a famous fortune teller with her.

"She will tell our fortunes, and we will know if we are meant to be together," she said.

Indeed, the time was nearing when luck and fortune were becoming paramount, and I was a bit superstitious about the fateful future.

Thus, we went to an area where wharfs and shanties crowded at the riverside. This was where holy items, like the red amulet that I wore, were sold. For generations, these amulets had been dug up, relics from the past, while others were still being manufactured and aged, so they appeared to be from a previous era.

The fortune tellers there teased out the futures of amulet buyers and recommended protective charms. For young lovers, this fortune telling was part of the thrill of first romance. For solitary older ladies, grown a little wrinkled, fortune telling could change their luck or perhaps help decide whether they should settle on a not-so-desirable man who had unaccountably turned his love to her. It was a place for making strategic decisions.

Rangsei and I moved through the vendors, shielded from the sun by low-hanging pieces of canvas which made the entire market dark and created a richly musty smell. The amulets stared at us as she led me confidently down an aisle that sloped towards the river. It was the dry season, but the river would still sometimes flood the market. The ground here was no longer cement but made up of planks laid down to cover the mud.

There were racks and racks of these amulets on every side, each in a little slot, ready to be seen and discussed by the vendors, who each regarded themselves as an expert. Each vendor had a magnifying loupe to examine an amulet and tell the potential buyer of its history and protective powers. Some amulets were specially blessed by notable hermits, monks, or even royal figures. Usually, they were presented like my red Buddha was, encased in a tiny triangular gold frame with glass on the front and back, protected from damage. Those who walked through the market often wore thick gold chains with multiple amulets hanging from them, each amulet to protect from a different aspect of the vicissitudes of life. It was another all intriguing, all impenetrable thing to consider.

"This is the one my friend told me about," Rangsei said. "This person is very true. She knows."

She pulled back the canvas tent-like door on an enclosed vendor's booth, and we entered.

Inside, we were greeted, not by anyone old or mysterious, but by a professional-looking woman with a keen gaze.

She was introduced as Professor May, "Professor" in this context being a word akin to "teacher." It was an honorific meant to denote the great regard with which her adherents held her. Her hair was puffed up and jet black, a throwback to the era of big-haired women of the past. She wore no makeup, but already had the ideal brown skin, rounded features, and long eyelashes that makeup was employed to create. Her sharply defined lips sat like a rind of orange, yet there was no hint of voluptuousness.

Rangsei said something to her in the local tongue and I instinctively realized I was to take out my red amulet, which I did. They spoke more together and Rangsei showed Professor May her own amulet that she wore around her neck, gifted to her by her father.

Finally, a set of cards was produced, somewhat like tarot cards, but they were cards from a local mystical tradition. We each drew one. Then there was more talking in the local language, and the lighting of joss sticks, which Rangsei and I held between our hands in a reverent *wai*.

Suddenly and without any preamble, Professor May began to speak to me in nearly perfect English.

"You've come from so very far away, yes. Here, yes here, is the place where you are now." A pause. "There is no longer any distance that separates you from your fate. You are here." A pause. "I don't know if you believe any of this," she added.

This was an apologetic statement, assuming I was a scientifically minded and opinionated Westerner who would be quick to point out that the beliefs of other cultures were mere superstitions to be scoffed at.

Rangsei broke in immediately saying, "Oh no, he believes it." I nodded politely and left it at that. Maybe I did. I wanted to.

Then I could feel Professor May focus on me as she spoke. I could feel her concentration and sincerity. I knew she was speaking in generalities and that this was her trade, but it was impressive.

Her "reading" of me: I loved my mother, and I had had a good childhood. Obvious things. I could see her watching me for my reactions, which I assumed I was broadcasting a moment before I responded.

She told me I was meant for great things, that people underestimated me, and that I would soon be rich.

Perhaps she had convinced herself she was psychic because, when the general things she said hit the ear of the listener, they did seem prescient. Yet, even knowing this, I still luxuriated in hearing that my destiny was at hand.

Finally, she got to the romantic aspect, concerning Rangsei and me and deep love, things we had not said out loud ourselves, so we both shyly looked at each other. Professor May spoke about honesty—about how honest I was—and how it made me the perfect mate for her and how we must share everything.

She showed us the cards, laying them out on the table and kindly explaining the significance of the mythological symbols on them. Halfway through, she abruptly stopped and gathered up the cards and started again, and then after this second time, appeared frustrated.

"This is unusual," she said, almost to herself. I had the ego to imagine that my greatness was interfering with the fall of cards that were used to telling the fortunes of mere trysting youngsters.

"I don't understand what is coming to me," she explained, "but this is the message." She paused and closed her eyes as if listening intently.

"Bert, I can see your past, where you are from, the life and the trials you have experienced. I can see your street, it is something like a tree, it is filled with trees. No, it's the name of a tree, wood, forest. It's Maple, Maplewood Avenue, you have come a long way from your home at Maplewood

Avenue." It was a throwaway line. She did not emphasize it. She rattled on, talking about more general and hopeful things to appeal to the emotions.

But I was momentarily stunned. I knew she could only have known the name of that street because I had written it on the entry card when I came into this country—my dummy address in the U.S.

Could it be that someone sought to impress me with the truth of my fate and fortune with this amazing information about my life? And the only way they could have come up with this was by pawing through piles of entry cards to find the one I filled out when entering the country.

They had found a bit of trivia which they thought was genuine. Yes, I was being watched. It had to be.

The fortune teller was explaining that Rangsei and I were meant to be together and must share everything. My mind was spinning, trying to calculate what was happening. She went on to stress that we must be honest with each other for our fates to be "fulfilled with happiness."

I knew that I was being keenly observed by Professor May, who could glean information about what I really thought from my least expression.

This all had to be a setup—unless Professor May was truly psychic and had somehow reached into the abyss of my mind and pulled out that street name. They—whoever they were—were trying a wondrously obtuse way to enchant me into honesty.

Instead, it was warning me that something was not right.

This meant someone was keeping an eye on me. It meant they must know something—our plot—was afoot. It would mean that Rangsei was in on it, bringing me here and encouraging me to be honest.

Our fortune telling session was over. We said our goodbyes. Rangsei smiled at me. She took my hand and led me out of the amulet market. I tried to smile at her like I always did. It was hard to really know a woman.

Rangsei stopped at a flower stand. She picked out a frangipani which I bought and placed in her hair. This was a delicately hued flower with thick petals. It was impossibly exotic—to me at least—but commonplace here, the sort of flower that begged to be placed in the hair of a beautiful woman.

Knowing what I knew now made me tired. It made me want to recede from the world. It made me feel a bit sorry for myself.

We walked down the street and entered a modest government exhibit of broken statue fragments from an earlier, grand empire. Among the stone things on display was a statue base with broken feet and a sign saying the rest of the statue had been stolen long ago. The sign was in the local language, and Rangsei read it out to me.

We ate rice and chicken at a streetside restaurant. We said little and neither of us admitted to the other what we were thinking. I said goodbye to her for the night. A barrier lowered within my mind to cut myself off from her.

5

It was the day before the big event. Our putsch would be conducted on Saturday morning when everyone was at home and businesses were closed. I was anxious for it to happen, as I was fearing someone was on to us or that people were blabbing, or both.

When I arrived for work that Friday, amped up for the final workday before the coup, Noi informed me that we were going over to the foreign ministry to finalize my working papers. This was good news, I thought. At least something about me would be legal. We rode over to the ministry while she gossiped about some staff she disapproved of.

Once in the ministry, we walked down the long, officious halls. We passed a group of men, uniformed bureaucrats. They looked at me as if they were sizing me up.

Suddenly, it bubbled up in my mind—they must know. Even if they did not know everything, they knew something, because the fortune teller was part of something much bigger. And Rangsei must be a part of it. It was all closing in on me. I would be exposed as a failure and a fool.

We passed a holding cell full of foreigners. I had heard of this—it was for visa overstayers and other minor scofflaws. It was a room with jail-like bars across the opening that fronted to the hall we were walking down. Inside, inmates lay on the floor or sat up, backs against the far wall. Most appeared to be the riffraff of neighboring countries—the scammers or troublemakers too dumb to properly skirt the law. A few miserable-looking Europeans. They noticed me and watched me as I walked past.

As we arrived at the interview room, Noi began complaining to me that no one else was called to the ministry and asked me what I had been up to. I probably went white, but I just shrugged my shoulders and said nothing. No turning back now. She looked at me with exaggerated skepticism, like I was disrupting her otherwise well-planned day.

Beside us, seated on a wooden bench, were four local police officers. Were they waiting to be told to arrest me, or just lounging indolently? I could not tell.

I was summoned into a room with a table and chairs—a dingy conference room.

I sat down and could immediately tell that the man seated at the table was one of the special locals who could deal with someone like me. He did not stand as I entered or show any fawning deference as I was used to. His bearing, his simple blue Western-style suit, the slight smirk on his face—indicated someone not at all hesitant to argue and confront a foreigner. He had the mottled, uneven skin and face of a tough, yet he looked at me in a friendly way and right in the eye, like a fellow Westerner. He then leaned back in his chair as if he already knew what he wanted to know.

As I had learned in Thailand, there is a different class of people in every country beyond the everyday ones who a tourist usually meets. These are those who had studied overseas, excelling in a foreign culture, while still retaining an appreciation of their own culture's ways when they returned to their homeland. Then, as one who can stand in between two disparate cultures, they had an almost shamanistic ability to deal with strange foreigners. They could parry with the wiliest Western diplomats while maintaining their own influence via their local cultural norms with their countrymen. Unlike the workaday men who regarded me as an impossible zoo animal, these elite men could see right through me. That's what I was afraid of.

The questioning began and it was a skeptical probing about my work experience and my past, what I was doing here, etcetera. It could have just been procedural, or there could have been more to it.

Every answer I gave was met with a momentary pause, as if to say, "I don't believe that." The pause invited me to say something else so that I might further convince him.

I held my tongue and answered the questions cheerily and directly and then ignored the pauses that were invitations to add more. The guilty man would try to overexplain, I knew.

He asked if I had been in contact with military men. This was the first dicey question. I defaulted to saying "No" pleasantly.

He asked about what kind of equipment I was working on at CLB. I explained about upgrading the broadcasting equipment there. "Good for the country," I added. I knew that the importation of technology into a country that had no hope of producing it was usually lauded here, but my questioner did not give any reaction.

Each time I answered a question, it was the same. The man's head rocked back almost imperceptibly with a sharp squinting of the eyes. It was a physical manifestation of not getting the further volunteering of incriminating information he was expecting.

As a little boy, I was taught in church that I did not want to lie. I believed it. But then, as I grew up, I saw that everyone lied—about mistakes made, about backing into a car, about declaring taxes. I realized that no one really believed that they should not lie. Still, my religious training made me a regretful liar—and I was never good at it.

So, during the interview, I felt my skin flush, and I wanted to fidget. I tried not to look around nervously. I thought of the fortune teller telling me about honesty.

But I resisted, and my answers, designed to protect my freedom and my future fortune, came easier and easier.

Finally, I was presented a list of questions—a declaration. It was on the peculiarly thin and cheap paper that was used in that country in those days. This paper always had an aged appearance, as if it had been pulled out of a filing cabinet where it had sat in the dark for many years, slowly retracting and crinkling.

It listed the business activities that CLB was permitted to be engaged in. It also listed what it was not permitted to do, which included a list of normally implausible things, such as arms dealing, espionage, and rebellion.

I checked the correct boxes, affirming I was only doing what I was supposed to and signed it. I started to feel cocky. I chuckled a bit at the list to show how crazy these things were for a lowly tech guy like me.

Then it was over. The man interviewing me seemed to be already considering his next interrogation. I no longer felt his attention. I exited the room and sat on a bench in the hallway while Noi attended to more paperwork in another office.

I silently assessed what had happened. I guess this meant the authorities did not know anything for certain—or at least the timeline of it. Would they have risked tipping me off by questioning me or were they sloppy functionaries who had no idea what was going on? Would the document I just signed be used to incriminate me later? Maybe signing the document would allow them to arrest me for lying, as they must know what was going on. But a list of things like this to sign was surely just boilerplate.

The soldier in the rain came into my mind. Someone must know. I had not thought about it since it had happened. Strange how your own mind protects you.

Remembering him, the man, felt like a weight bearing down on me, and, as I sat in the brightly lit hall, I realized no one could know this but me.

Noi rejoined me with folders of documents. As we exited, the police officers sitting there looked at me one more time, mournfully, I thought, wishing they could arrest me. Maybe I imagined too much. I was not sure anymore at that point. I kept a pleasant look on my face.

Noi again complained that I "caused trouble" and that the extra time and paperwork was annoying. I told her I did not know anything about it and tried to look relaxed. I guess this meant that Noi had no idea what was being planned at CLB. She said my working documents and my passport were now finalized and would be returned to CLB soon. This was all good.

In the taxi going back to CLB, she yammered on about the trouble getting work permits in general for the foreign workers at CLB and I pretended to listen and be interested in her problems.

6

I returned to the control room. I could no longer see the bags of money behind the console, and I knew why. I peeked over and they were down to the last two. We were ready. It felt exciting, like the last day of school.

The events at the ministry had made what we were planning more real. I sat down, realizing I was trembling a bit in excitement and agitation. Mike entered the room, and I pulled myself together.

"You did good, kid," he said, as if he knew exactly what had transpired during my meeting at the ministry.

"Thanks," I said stoically, like it was both an ordeal but no big deal because I was tough. Behind Mike, Amnuay appeared. Amnuay motioned for Ganju to leave, which he did.

"Do you think they know anything?" Mike asked.

"It didn't seem like they did. A few general questions and signing a paper," I said. "They questioned me like they suspected something, maybe, but I don't know for sure. They probably would have suspicions anyway in dealing with Chiang, right?"

Amnuay and Mike exchanged glances.

"They sometimes do this, for an American," Amnuay said. "Sometimes." He said it like he was not sure.

"Did they ask about anything specific?" Mike said.

"No. It was nothing specific," I said. "Just boilerplate stuff about the nature of my job and what I was doing. That's what it seemed to me. They might have suspicions, but I don't think they know the timeline. I mean, when it will happen. Had I not been... well, doing what we are doing here, I wouldn't have thought anything of what they were asking."

Both Amnuay and Mike were silent, calculating in their minds.

Amnuay turned to Mike. "It doesn't sound like they know, not precisely," he said. "No, I don't think they have a clue," he continued, saying it with a questioning tone.

The soldier I had fought with in the rain returned from the guilty part of my mind.

"What about the soldier...?" I could not say more, and I did not want to say anything more out loud.

"People disappear all the time," Mike answered. "Those military cliques are always in conflict with each other over business and turf and all sorts of things involving money. It's likely they think their man is in custody at another base, eventually to be released. This goes on all the time."

"There's no imminent chatter," Amnuay added. "I think you're right. They suspect, but don't know anything for sure. All of this proves it. But it's lucky we are ready, and it will be over soon. Anyway, it's in motion already and it will happen." He said this like we should be impressed at his leadership. He was not smoking, but he moved his hand absentmindedly, as if he wanted to be holding a cigarette.

My experience with the fortune teller only strengthened the idea that there had to be suspicions. I was still pondering how Rangsei was part of it, a plant to keep track of me or make me spill information. Maybe Amnuay was right, they did not know of any imminent plan. Yet I said nothing about the fortune teller, as I did not want to reveal how innocently dumb I had been in getting involved with Rangsei.

We quickly went over the details of my part of the mission the next day—I would leave with a convoy of APCs from the friendly base, along with Tieng to assist me, on our way to capture the Lion's Den and the communications hub there.

Some part of my mind told me I was just an English teacher from Bangkok. Maybe the voice was Andrew's, nestled in the school break room back in Bangkok, who would somehow know what I was on the verge of doing. And I knew he would disapprove of the perfidy of it all, and that I could dare break from the clutches of easy work in Bangkok that would whittle away his years with no respite.

I nodded grimly as I discussed this with Amnuay and Mike like I was a seasoned military man, or rather, like I was a determined freebooter.

Then Mike briefed us on his mission—rallying his local associates, young toughs on motorcycles en masse, to cut communications at a tower in another part of town. These were of the "informal economy," men running gambling dens, the illegal lottery, and the lowly, underpaid police that facilitated these places.

The communications tower that was their target was not normally strategic, so it would only be lightly guarded, but it could be an alternate means of command and control for army units in other parts of the country if Thaw Kai's comms were out of action, thus, it had to be seized as well.

Amnuay explained, in hushed tones, that various cliques of military men were entering the town tonight to back up the putsch, but to trust only our white-pinned brigade. He also instructed me to take the special radios home with me tonight and go directly to the staging area tomorrow.

"Don't come back here until it is done. If there are any difficulties, regroup at the safe house—that's the annex." This was the annex where I had set up the radiation cone and met the officer who mistook me for John.

"Stay around this area," Mike told me. "They'll keep track of us even if they aren't sure. It will all be better once it is done." This was a rare admission of everyone's stress. I was glad I did not hear this before I had gone to the ministry.

"Everything is going good, going to plan," Mike continued, as if to reassure us both. "Before long, it is all going to come together, and it is going to be great. You'll see."

It was an almost magically encouraging sentiment. His voice was rich and fulsome. Even Amnuay looked hopeful. Yeah, I thought. We were all going to be rich.

Mike and Amnuay exited and Ganju returned. He looked at me and nodded his grim baby face in approval, I guess for my performance at the ministry. Even he knew.

It made me worry because people always talk too much. Few have the skills to hold their information close, particularly when success seems certain.

Our march to the Lion's Den was only a fragment of what was to happen. It was a culmination of a thousand desires— for power, for revenge, for ambition.

In my head I was going over all the items I would have to carry and all the tasks I would have to do on the day of action tomorrow. I did not write anything down. My task was to reroute and install communications equipment. Soldiers with me would be ready to disable radio towers and transmission equipment we could not co-opt. All from inside the prime minister's Lion's Den. It was an incredible thing to dare.

I had made careful plans. I packed all the secure radios, telephones, and the tools I needed to set up secure communications at the Lion's Den in a large backpack. The backpack was the cheap kind so many backpackers used when they flitted about the region. It looked about right for a foreigner like me to be carrying.

That my passport was at the ministry was emerging in my mind as a dire complication. I could not leave the country if I needed to. Maybe it was easier because I could not back out now. The decision was made.

Later that day, I noticed all the bags of money were gone, as was Ganju. Curious, I walked out the back door and over to the signal house. Its door was uncharacteristically ajar, and I looked inside. It was a scene of abandonment. Whatever listening equipment was once inside was gone, as were Don and John. They knew something was happening. I guess most everyone must know by now.

On this day of all days, when I was leaving to go home with a backpack full of radios, Noi stopped me at the front reception area and began to discuss paperwork that might be needed to further verify something for my working papers. I thought to myself that the government would soon be acting on my behalf.

I chuckled inwardly and said yes to everything she was saying, and she soon realized I was not paying attention. She stopped talking and put her hands on her hips in an exaggerated, but serious manner. I replied with "I'll do it later." She gave me a very cross look. I said, "I'm late" and broke away, and she never questioned my backpack, instead angry that my inattention impinged on her sense of importance.

The great day was upon me, and if it all went to plan, it would be over before anyone could stop us.

7

I had already determined not to get caught with the secure radio equipment in my room, so I tossed the backpack up on top of a metal shed that abutted my apartment. This was completely out of sight of everyone. A tree, dripping with sap, sagged over the metal roof, so the backpack was entirely invisible. It might be stolen, but I was more worried about getting caught with it in my room, in case this whole thing fell apart, so I took the chance of leaving it there.

It was good that I did, because she was waiting there for me, alone, in the lobby of the apartment, on the old vinyl sofa that was part of every lobby in the city. I sat down beside her quickly before she could get up, as I did not want her up in my apartment that night.

"Are you okay?" Rangsei said kindly. "My friend saw you at the ministry."

"Yeah, I'm okay. It's just for my work permit. They are making it now."

"I see," she replied. She was trying to get information from me. I wished we had never visited the fortune teller. I did not want to know this about her. However, I was now too close to doom or glory. Magic could make no difference to me anymore.

"So, what's really going on?" she said. Her hand was on her chest, right where her amulet would be. "Remember what the fortune teller said? You are lucky, and our future?"

"Yes," I said.

"We should share everything." Then, looking deep into my eyes, "I know something's going on."

My blood ran cold for just a moment, but I recovered.

"I was there because of my work permit," I said with a kind of simplicity like there was nothing more to be explained.

"Don't do this to me," she said. "I know you are sincere. I always knew that." She started to cry. It was not dramatic. Just a girl crying.

Her words and tears still touched me, but I did not realize this until I found myself holding her hand, one of my palms under it and one on top. I was shocked I had done this involuntarily and I quickly pulled away, letting her hand drop onto her lap.

I could see in her eyes that she somehow sensed every step of my feelings, and I thought to myself: this is a special person, but then, no, this is a betrayer. I wished we were different people in some other reality, far from this place.

"Let's go to the park on Sunday, okay?" I said, taking the initiative.

"Really?" she said.

"Yes, I'll tell you everything then."

Her insistence instantly dissolved. I knew this meant she did not know the timing of the coup. By Sunday, it would have already happened.

"We can talk about everything then," she added hopefully, as if to confirm my commitment.

I repeated that I would see her on Sunday, not inviting her up to my room. She said goodbye and left. She knew something and they knew something, but not when. It hardened me, the smiling part of me. There is one inside and one outside, and I smiled in both places.

I thought of Rangsei and all the things she had said to me. I imagined calling her back and telling her everything. What a fool this emotion makes me. She would wait for me on Sunday, but it would already be too late. Our march to the Lion's Den and a new government for her would be complete. I wished that she was apart from the scheme—apart from my fantasy of becoming a rich man. She could have been part of the prize. Grateful to be with someone like me.

I went up to my room and placed the chair under the doorknob. As I carelessly dragged it to the door, it put a gash in the linoleum-like floor covering, and, oddly enough, I was suddenly more worried about the damage I had caused rather than being involved in what would happen tomorrow.

I thought I should write down what I knew, perhaps mail it back home so there was a record if I turned up dead or in jail. I made an outline and notes of what we were doing. It did not make much sense in its abbreviated form, but I was too tired to go on. It was too late to mail anything anyway. There I was with my notes about the scheme—my only insurance—barricaded in my room.

"You fool. That will not keep anyone out," I thought to myself, as I regarded the chair leaning against the door.

Then a flood of alternate thoughts flooded in. I should get out of here. I should tell Rangsei I knew everything, and she did not.

I thought of the miserable foreigners entangled by dodgy businesses in far-off lands—locked up, thrown out of helicopters, or gunned down in the street. Or, more typically, those who were found dead in their meager city apartments like mine. The police would say it was suicide, and their family would spend a small fortune on investigations to try to prove what everyone already knew—that their boy had been consumed by something he had underestimated.

I took a cold-water shower—the water was extra cold that night— as I continued to think about what I was about to do. This was my legend. I was making it. I already had a pretty good story and I had come this far.

I paced about my room as if to expend some of the psychic energy that had built up. I checked that the chair was still firm, leaning up against the doorknob.

Looking down, I noticed an envelope had been slid under the door. Inside was a note. It was on the same thin wrinkly paper that I had seen at the ministry. Written in clear and crisp handwriting, it read, "Leave this country within 24 hours."

So, I had 24 hours more. There would be no cowering, no tearfully admitting everything. It was going to happen, and I wanted to do it. Before 24 hours was out, I would know for sure what was to be. They would know too.

I was doing something seditious and valuable, all down to what I could get out of it and what I could get away with. Is this not the dream of any young man? I would try, and there was no reason to believe anything except that I was here, and I was making it happen.

People I would never know were coming home to their lives on the street below. The sun was setting on this day, the only day of its kind there was, and I was getting excited.

It was one of those fretful nights, when sleep finally came from long exhaustion, after the fires of the mind burned through every scenario, again and again.

PART V

1

It was Saturday. I could tell something was different when I woke up that morning. It was quiet. No rush. Everything was paused for a restful day. This is what we were counting on. Officials were at home or out of contact. People slept late. Once Monday came around, the news of what we had done would have been digested and the new path of the nation would be clear. This was going to happen.

I retrieved the backpack of equipment, still safely on the metal roof, covered with morning dew. I found a motorcycle taxi that brought me over to our friendly military base.

When I arrived, the main gates were open. I walked inside and no one was at the guard post. The place was deserted. Maybe I was late again. Maybe they had left without me. Maybe it was all beyond me, an English teacher from Bangkok. Maybe I had imagined it all.

Then, walking towards me, as if appearing out of the bright sunlight itself, was the CLB groundskeeper Phong, scowling and with a mongrel dog following after him. This time he held a rifle, and he was holding it like a sensible soldier and pointing it directly at me. He was lucid and hostile and gestured with his gun like a pitchfork, as if telling me to leave.

I stood my ground as I began to sense a rumbling, maybe near, maybe far, of machines gurgling, the deep sounds from the mysterious reactions inside engines. Ganju, along with several soldiers, came through the second gate of the base, scanning the area. Ganju was dressed in black fatigues. When he saw me, he gestured at me to follow him. I took one last look at Phong. He looked disappointed as he lowered his gun.

I jogged out the side entrance and around the back of the base to an alley. This is where the hum was coming from. A line of APCs was there with soldiers milling around and preparing themselves for the trek to the Lion's Den. Two of the vehicles towed mobile generators in case we needed our own power. It was an impressive convoy. I handed out the secure radios from my backpack, warning the soldiers not to change the channels which I had carefully selected and taped down. Seeing everything, I thought we could not lose.

Amnuay was tensely surveying the convoy. He was out of his normal work clothes and into khaki pants and a green polo shirt, as if ready for a spirited weekend in the country. He looked uneasy and out of his element, like he was fulfilling the role of an office manager checking that the proper requisition paperwork was filled out.

Tieng, also dressed in black fatigues, was moving among the men confidently, with a huge silver gun strapped to his hip. The retiring, feminine aspect of his bearing was gone, and he radiated a ready-for-anything swagger.

"I'm ready," he said to me blankly when he saw me.

I was proud of him. He was secretly a tough guy.

I was seated within the second APC with Ganju. Also with us was a team of five others—all older, with steely gazes. I had asked about this in the planning stages and been assured all the soldiers on this mission would be "specialists," not the young or fat soldiers I was used to seeing. I wanted to make sure we could do the job.

Ganju saw me regarding the soldiers and said, "Strike team. For the Lion of the country," with a little mirthless smile. He then made a slicing gesture across his neck.

Had I asked for this when I asked for "specialists?" Had I asked for soldiers to kill the prime minister? It was suddenly both a horrifying and thrilling thought, but it was too late now for anything to be rethought. Probably had to be done. It was all or nothing. The convoy lurched forward and a wall of sound from the engine rattled us.

Amnuay was not coming along, of course, as he was one of the big company bosses. Still, he looked pale and worried as the convoy passed him.

Spotting me, he said, "Good luck, American," somehow both sincerely and sarcastically. He nervously flicked his cigarette as we rolled away.

It was Ganju, Tieng, and me and the local soldiers— against a whole nation. And Mike elsewhere targeting a communications tower. I was part of an exclusive group indeed—those who knew.

And it was serious, targeting Prime Minister Thaw Kai, a man I had shaken hands with not long ago. But I tried not to think of that. There would be plenty of time for that later when it was all done.

To lighten my mood, I said quietly to Tieng, who was seated next to me, "I wonder what Chiang is doing now?" Tieng shook his head, as if I should not mention Chiang by name.

I knew Chiang himself never took chances. He would be already safely out of the country. He would let those who were ambitious and willing, like Tieng, like me, take the chance on his behalf.

Tieng patted the gun on his hip. "Someday I will assign others to do it, but today, I have to take the risk myself."

This impressed me. Seeing his bearing and his gun, I wanted to hear the story of who he really was, and how he could so easily shift gears from his everyday persona to this tough guy I first witnessed today. But the roaring engine sounds of the APC convoy and my thoughts of what was coming drowned out my curiosity.

The convoy moved through the Saturday morning city. Soldiers peeked out the top hatch of each vehicle and others were seated on top in a casual manner, happily enjoying the cool morning air. There could hardly have been a more conspicuous sight, but the shutters and curtains of the surrounding buildings were still closed that morning.

We passed the long-abandoned U.S. Embassy. It made me think of my country where men rarely, if ever, got on the backs of military trucks and went off to overthrow their government. A local guard in a hammock in front of the embassy rocked gently.

"That is where I came from," I thought.

The embassy had been closed for years, as most were during the former times of war. A new embassy would arise in a few years.

It was on these streets that rebels had once marched. It was events I had read of long ago, events that had lured me to adventure, to take a chance on my fortune. And now I was here on these streets myself.

I recalled that the diplomatic services of the U.S. and other Western nations were currently being conducted from a suite of hotel rooms somewhere else in the city. I imagined the embassy tea parties they held in air-conditioned rooms, and I wondered if any of them guessed what was going on, right now.

Once out of town, we crossed a small watercourse on the road to the Lion's Den. Perhaps it was a roaring river after the rainy season, but now it was just a modest creek. The extent of the annual flooding could be determined by the size of the massive, pitched bridge that spanned the watercourse. Before we crossed, the column came to a halt. All the soldiers peeked out of the windows expectantly and more climbed out of the APCs and joined those already on top. A soldier from the head of the column opened the door of our vehicle and looked around. Spotting me, he said something in broken English (as if I was someone who needed to know), while ignoring everyone else. Then he slammed the door and shouted an order.

I did not understand what he said, so one of the soldiers explained. "This is the boundary. This soldier clique must not cross the river," he said. The vehicles crawled forward onto the bridge.

"And yet we are," I said to myself.

"Yes," Ganju said. "This is breaking the law. South of the river is Thaw Kai's men. Only the PM."

It was the boundary between military factions. Now, conflict would be inevitable.

I suddenly thought that, if this went wrong, the foreigner, the American freebooter, would certainly be offered up as the scapegoat. It was true, but I told myself it meant I could not fail.

We were passing through startlingly green rice fields. In the dry part of the year, it was all brown, like a burned land. But now it was the rice-growing season and green was burning across the fields. Every turn of the head and every bend of the road exposed more greenness. In places, as men were wont to do, the land was upturned, scarred by plows exposing a pungent redness, almost to a blood red.

We plodded along a watercourse by the road where legions of waterwheels spun endlessly, each raising water into an adjacent rice field. Shacks sat on the banks of the river, and before most was a farmer and his wife who gently regarded the passing convoy. Dust grew and grew, as even the main roads out of town like this were only dirt. I could taste it in my teeth after a while. It was a far cry from the air-conditioned van that took me to the Lion's Den the first time.

Surely, Thaw Kai could feel that something was heading towards him.

2

We roared right up to the gates of the Lion's Den, now closed. There was not another vehicle on the road or a soldier standing guard. Maybe the compound was already deserted. Maybe they were waiting for us.

The lead APC burst through the gate. It was breathtaking. This was the very symbol of revolution and adventuring in these places, like the capture of the U.S. Embassy in Saigon and the horrible glories of revolution.

The first two APCs—with me in the second one—continued on to the gates that encircled Thaw Kai's private residence. These gates were left open, and I was disappointed not to re-experience the sensation of crashing through them. Other APCs fanned out through the rest of the complex.

I quickly picked out the transmission towers looming over Thaw Kai's house in the background. This was my target.

We piled out of our vehicles at Thaw Kai's mansion. The front door was ajar, giving the impression that the place had been hurriedly evacuated. The soldiers, along with Tieng, Ganju and myself, entered with an odd air of respect. We paused at the entryway carefully. It was dark and silent. No air-con on, but it was still a bit cool, as if it had not been long since it had been running. Specks of dust were rising in the air and a single shaft of white light from outside fell through a high window. The rest was in daylight shadow.

The Cupid statue stood on the end of a balustrade with its creepy, mocking smile. It seemed to notice us, as if saying,

"I see what you are doing." I thought of knocking it down, or, even better, taking one of the soldier's rifles and shooting it to pieces. Instead, not a word was spoken, and we thundered up the stairway to the second floor in search of the communications room.

One of the men had a floorplan of the house, but I pointed out the way to the men, having been there before. We moved along the wide upstairs hallway past grand rooms.

The door to Thaw Kai's office was locked and it was a substantial door—one that looked, at first glance, to be a normal door, but that was really vault-like.

"Get a crowbar on this," I ordered Tieng. One of the men who came with us, nicknamed "Toolie," was carrying a full complement of tools, and he and Tieng started working on the door as Ganju and I continued down the hall.

We came to a double door at the end of the hall. Beyond this, the blueprint showed the bedrooms of Thaw Kai and his rarely seen wife.

The soldiers were whispering. Ganju leaned to me and whispered, "They think Thaw Kai is still in the house."

We entered this suite of rooms through a short entry hall with locked doors to other rooms, perhaps to house a guard or a valet. Straight on, we came to the main grand bedroom. It had clearly been decorated by a woman. Its monumental bed with a canopy reached up into a recessed ceiling—all in ruffles and salmon pink. A bench seat was at the end of the bed and on one side of the room was an ornate princess mirror and a place to apply makeup. On the right was a door to the wardrobe and bathroom.

Members of our group fanned out, some moving into adjacent rooms. I went through a door on the left side of the room. It led to a large closet filled with men's clothes—rows of identical blue suits and white shirts, exactly what a prime minister would need for his continual public appearances. Beyond that, a lavatory, this one a man's, with aftershave and cologne and a hairbrush matted with hair. A mannequin head was crowned with a lush hairpiece. Thaw Kai clearly did not wear one—his thinning hair was apparent—but this showed he was thinking about it. Seeing this made me sad, as we were rummaging through a man's house. Seeing these things made him real, not just a hectoring voice on TV. I pocketed the hairbrush. I did not know why; it was just a weird souvenir.

Through another door was finally the lair of the man himself. I entered carefully and strangely felt that Thaw Kai could appear at any moment, remember me and sneer, and I could tell him this was all a mistake.

It was not a large room, but it contained all the clutter of items that showed it was his working office. There were trophies and plaques, and all manner of stuffed heads on the wall—antelope-type animals and endangered forest cattle. I had never wanted to kill dumb animals, but there was something primally attractive about possessing such trophies. Maybe it made men feel they could capture the very spirit of their prey by sequestering the once living heads within their living quarters.

Piles of books were jammed onto shelves, and many were stacked on the floor. I knew that Thais, as well as those of this nation, had a prohibition against leaving books on the floor, as it was thought to dishonor the books, as books gave knowledge. This came from a time when books were an expensive rarity and likely to be chewed to pieces by termites. But Thaw Kai must have been a voracious reader and was not shy, at least in this private workspace, of piling his books wherever he wanted to.

In the center of the room sat a messy desk. It was not anything like the massive desk that I had seen during the party and that was meant to impress Chiang, but a working desk where a man would think and create. In a corner of the room was a queen-sized bed, probably used as a day bed, I thought, for taking naps.

Tieng entered and started going through drawers and gathering up paperwork and directing a soldier with a camera to photograph the room. Chiang wanted all the paperwork we could find, especially contracts or agreements related to Chiang's business dealings or his rivals.

Suddenly, Ganju burst in with several men through an adjoining door, like police entering a danger zone, guns at the ready and alert. They were the strike team, looking for Thaw Kai. They lowered their weapons when they saw who we were. We had been careless in wandering about and were nearly shot.

White plastic tubs were brought in. Files and paperwork were dumped in and carried away—unopened mail, a few packages, and some thick official-looking dossiers. I wondered what secrets they might contain about Thaw Kai and Chiang. A small safe was located by his desk and carried off. It felt like we were thieves.

Then, on the far side of the room, I saw what I was looking for. It was the door to the communications room. The door was slightly ajar, and I could see inside it was a room shielded against eavesdropping, just like I had seen at the annex.

I looked in. It was a tiny room with a single table and chair and a radio console on the table with microphones, clearly for Thaw Kai's use. Another door was open on the other side. I could see that this led to Thaw Kai's formal office where we had met him at the party, and he had jousted with Chiang. I guess he had sealed his fate then.

Something made me pause at the door. This was too easy, and the house was deserted. I stopped one of the soldiers who was going to push past me into the room.

I kneeled down to take a look for a second. There, at ankle-level, was a thick, black wire. I pointed this out to the soldier, who gasped audibly. It was a booby trap.

The soldier called out to his men. I stepped back, shaken. We had run all over the house like wild men without a thought and it had almost got me, right here. I sat down in Thaw Kai's chair.

I looked out over his desk, then thought that I probably should not touch anything.

Ganju soon came to me, holding up a wired device, somewhat carelessly.

"Little booby trap," he said.

"This means something," I said to him. "They know and had time to set this up."

I looked around, feeling we were being watched.

I cautiously entered the communications room. Several soldiers were already there.

All the wires to the radios had been cut.

"This isn't right," I said. "There's nothing we can do from here now. We have to get to the array out back."

The soldiers were looting the house now, going through cabinets and drawers and gathering up the odds and ends that they found.

"Hey, stop that!" I shouted. "We have a job to do." One of the soldiers, who clearly did not understand what I was saying, looked at me with a confused smile as he rifled through a drawer.

I ran out of the suite of rooms to the main hall. I found a room off the hallway that housed items of worship—multi-limbed red elephants, golden Buddhas, white Buddhas with undulating waves emanating from them, a monkey god, a fat cat waving its arm endlessly, an emaciated forest hermit, and masks representing characters from the Ramakien. Along the side wall of the chamber there were photos of deceased loved ones—a grandmother, an aunt perhaps, and an old, shriveled man looking out through the blurry photo as if he was surprised.

I had seen many houses with something like this, a pantheon of the sacred within one's own residence. Both the poor and rich maintained one if they could. The richer one was, the grander it could be. The utility of it could be as varied as the items themselves—different kinds of luck for love, for business, for turning away the dragons of chaos, and for placating the spirit of the land itself, which predated all else.

The room had a circular window. I gently stepped behind the shelves that held the statues. I noted ruefully that I had my shoes on—shoes that should have been removed when we entered the residence, much less when we were stepping around venerated objects. This made me chuckle to myself, as this bit of social propriety was the least of the transgressions we were seeking to commit.

Out the window, I could see the backyard of the house, then a high barbed-wire fence, a steep ravine filled with trees, and then the communications array on the far side of that.

We had no prior knowledge that the communications towers were separated like this from Thaw Kai's house. We would have to get over there immediately.

My mind started to race—if there was no way to communicate from here, if Thaw Kai had escaped, if the place was deserted... all this pointed to a scary conclusion. Maybe I needed to find a place to hide out or even escape the country.

I went out into the hall and found Tieng and told him we had to get going to the communications towers right away. I wondered what all that money that was spread around had bought. I could see that we had been sloppy and overconfident, not knowing the communications towers could not be accessed directly from Thaw Kai's house.

I went back downstairs. The house was in chaos now, with soldiers carting various items out, looting the place of its bric-a-brac. Smiling men carried George V-style chairs and tables and other ornate furniture that was oddly popular with the ruling classes in the region.

The group of soldiers I had entered with, as well as Tieng, reassembled, and we tramped through a kitchen area. It was a double kitchen, as was the custom in extravagant houses. One was a show kitchen, pristine, for the family to get snacks from imported wooden cabinets. I walked through this kitchen as soldiers opened cabinets, examining the foreign-made packaged foods as if they were alien artifacts.

The adjoining working kitchen had cheaper white wooden cabinetry. This was where the smells and the oil from daily cooking were, where the house cook fried up masses of rice and vegetables and meats in metal woks over open flames, flinging the contents into the air and catching them as part of the cooking process. This spread microscopic droplets of cooking oil over the floor and ceiling. Over time, the oil formed a film on every surface, and this was why the dual kitchen was the right approach for those who could afford it, as it preserved the main show kitchen from the wear and tear of daily cooking.

Then, from a corner broom closet, a panicked man burst out. He had a rifle and began emptying it into the room.

Maybe the gods conspired to bend his aim to prevent a kill shot. Maybe the gods were asleep and did not guide his aim at all. Whatever it was, none of us were hit and one of the bullets went between me and a soldier next to me, hitting a narrow pillar separating two windows behind us with a sharp ping.

I started and grimaced. The soldiers with me snapped to presentness. Tieng grabbed the man and tried to knock his gun away, but he held his rifle firmly.

The shooter looked terrified and furious. He was clearly a cook or some other household staff, a wrinkled and baffled member of the servant underclass. He thought he was doing his duty, maybe, defending his boss's home. Tieng held him for only a moment, then pushed him back. The man stumbled back against the cabinets and started to raise his rifle again. Tieng pulled out his own gun in a single smooth confident motion and shot him.

There was no time to gasp. The man went down with the barest and most remote grunt. Our ears rang from the gunshot as he landed with a slap on the marble floor. No blood was visible, but I thought I could see a momentary mist of blood over his body. Then I could taste it, the aerated blood in this small space, along with gunpowder.

Tieng exchanged glances with us all and returned his pistol to its holster with satisfaction. Not many times one gets to shoot someone and be a tough guy about it.

"Good job," was all I could say, putting on my stoniest face, although I was reeling inside.

I exited the kitchen. I was not really scared then, but somehow, I knew I would be one day. Not of seeing the fool of a loyal man die in front of me, but of wondering about the few centimeters between me and the gunshot, wondering how one step slower, one moment faster, a surer aim, and it would have taken me. My end would have been right then. That was the thing that kept cads and heroes alike awake in years hence, long after their main adventures ended. The moment, its choices and the dumb, unconscious ones, would one day harry me awake in the dead of night.

3

Once outside at the front of the house, soldiers were standing around with no sense of urgency. This made me worry. The only thing that mattered was getting the communications going.

I exited out the gate from Thaw Kai's house into the wider compound. Several APCs and lots of military men were there. It was all calm and peaceful. I was not quite sure why there was no urgency. Maybe it was assumed that the putsch was a success. We had taken over the place without resistance. The prime minister and his soldiers had fled.

"Let's get one of those APCs going! Let's drive through the fence at the back right now!" I was fired up. I wanted to get this over with. It was time to get this going and get to the communications array.

I looked for the commander from our column but could not find him.

A group of soldiers walked towards me—an older commander and five other men behind him. Oddly, they did not look friendly, and I did not recognize them. The older man came right up to me while putting on a broad beret, as if he were preparing to say something official. He was a square flat-headed man with a close, military-style crewcut, probably worn since he entered the army. He was dark and wrinkled with a fat neck and a no-nonsense stare. It almost seemed like the men with him wanted to reach out and touch me but were hesitating. Then I saw the insignias on their uniforms and my heart sank. They were not the white unit pins of our friendly base, but maroon pins.

I looked around. There were indeed too many military vehicles here now. These could not all be from our convoy. Another military clique was involved.

I could sense a phalanx of men coming up from behind me. I was surrounded. The men looked from one to the other as if unsure who would give the order to arrest me.

Ganju and some of our soldiers exited the gates of the prime minister's residence carrying white tubs of documents. The new soldiers ran up and knocked the tubs out of their hands, scattering the paperwork across the ground. Then they roughly disarmed Ganju and his men. The papers on the ground began to slowly blow around the compound like confetti.

This signaled to the men surrounding me that they could act. All the soldiers, including the one facing me, raised weapons. It was both respectful and determined. I raised my hands as I saw Ganju and the other soldiers escorted over to me at gunpoint.

Tieng was led over to us at gunpoint as well, hands raised. One of the soldiers escorting him had Tieng's large silver handgun in his hand. Tieng had a disdainful look on his face and had his eyes glued on the gun in the soldier's hand, clearly annoyed that it had been taken from him.

The doors of the APCs that we had arrived in were flung open and the contents rummaged through with suspicion. Our men were being disarmed and seated in rows near the front gate of the compound. It was happening politely and nearly silently. I wondered if this was done gently because all the soldiers had a common loyalty to each other while playing this game of cliques with politicians and businessmen who sponsored them.

Our soldiers waited in the ever-increasing heat as their hands were laboriously tied with makeshift pieces of pink twine that were rolled off a stiff bundle. One of the detained soldiers even offered his own pocketknife when the twine became hard to cut.

Ganju, Tieng, and I stood beside an APC. Ganju and I betrayed no emotion on our faces, but Tieng had his bottom lip stuck out like a petulant child, eyes still on his confiscated gun, held in a rucksack by one of our captors.

We were directed into an APC, along with a few of the soldiers in our group, their hands bound and now showing wide-eyed expressions of fear. It was clear we were the elite prisoners of the bunch, the foreigners, as our hands were not tied as the rest were.

I could see Ganju's baby face through his tattoos and battle-ready expression. I could almost hear him say, "I already know doom. It sits on my head smiling." He looked at me grimly, but good-naturedly. We had to think this was sort of fun or at least a challenge, but it was really neither.

Tieng's face had reverted to its Thai placidity. I guess we were all deep in thought, considering our next move. No use worrying about what had happened. Everything was on the line.

A large, professional-looking soldier got inside with us. He had a bushy mustache, uncharacteristic for a military man here. His unit pin was brown, denoting the prime minister's faction. He sat in a fold-down jump seat guarding the side exit door of the APC compartment we were all confined in.

I noted Ganju surreptitiously sizing him up. I could almost hear him thinking, "Could I get by this guy without being shot?" I considered this as well. He was bigger than I was, but I might have to try it.

4

Perhaps it would all be blamed on me, the foreign mercenary, and that would be quite an epitaph, but I was not ready to give up yet. We rumbled along back towards the city. Fear was rising. I would have to try to escape, at least give it a try. I did not want to end up regretting I had not taken one more chance. Luckily, my hands were not bound. This was the last chance before spending years detained or in legal limbo, if not executed.

I could see the long line of vehicles and soldiers out the back window. It would be hard to get away. Ganju and I exchanged glances. I was sure we were thinking the same thing. I continued running scenarios in my head.

Tieng still looked annoyed at his situation. He had tried to talk to the soldiers in the local language, trying to make a deal, but they refused to talk to him.

The other soldiers who were in our APC looked around in terror and spoke in whispers among themselves. Ganju and Tieng and I had made a choice to come out here on this day, but these soldiers, their hands tied with twine, were fodder. They were scared but also grinning in horror like beaten dogs trying to elicit sympathy. They were only following orders. I knew that their terror indicated the high degree of risk we were all facing once we were delivered to an unfriendly military base. I was hopeful that a common camaraderie among soldiers would win out over any retribution.

At that moment, our APC and four others cut off from the main convoy to an adjacent road.

"Why are we splitting off?" Tieng said. His voice was worried, and it made me worried.

"Maybe we are the higher-value prisoners," I said. "The ones they can blame it on and not have to blame the low-ranking soldiers." I did not know, but it seemed right. Ganju remained in a state of readiness, as if he already knew this, his eyes intent on some far-off thing.

Tieng again started to negotiate with the mustachioed guard. Each knew some of the other's language. He took charge like he was a businessman negotiating a deal. They were trying to find the common words from both their languages. At one point they both nodded, agreeing on an English translation of something. The word both were looking for was "failed."

Our putsch had failed. The guard laughed, this time at us. Tieng continued to try to speak to him, but the guard was continually shaking his head, as if he had no power over the matter.

I wondered about the guard's mustache. It was unusual for a soldier. Maybe he was an influential man, close to Thaw Kai, extra loyal and thus used for special purposes like this. Maybe this made him too big and consequential to be forced to shave his mustache.

I took stock of where we were. There were two armed men from the opposing camp standing on the back of the APC. In the front seats of the vehicle, there were probably at least two more men sitting up there beside the driver—it was hard to see for sure. Plus, the guard in the cab with us. It was a tricky situation.

It went quiet again, but soon I was exchanging questioning glances with Ganju. Psychically, we were saying to each other, "We must take action, but what? Should we jump out and run across the countryside?" I could see every intersecting watercourse and trail that led away from the road. Where could I run to? To a farmhouse shanty on stilts with some old granny inside? Or maybe I would stumble through the canals and rice fields and hide behind the gently turning water wheels. I looked to Ganju and decided he was unsure as well.

Maybe they would get rid of us to cover it up. There were legions of deaths from people riding motorcycles here every day, and it would be easy to tell someone that a drunken foreigner died in this far-off land falling afoul of the roads. No one would ever suspect the things I had done. That might be for the best.

As we rode along, there grew a sadness, a cringing feeling of regret connected to ambition and guilt and death. It was the feeling of having won the wrong thing by making the wrong choices on purpose. Of having every advantage in the world and voluntarily choosing one that hurt others. Maybe this was the right thing to think, but I had to steel myself to self-preservation. Self-doubt had to wait. It would come back soon enough in the future, one way or another.

I tried to reason it out. I was not tied up and we were still in the countryside. I knew I did not want to be delivered to an enemy military base where all bets were off. I imagined these third worlders and their interrogations. I imagined calling out in my pain that I wanted a lawyer. That almost made me laugh out loud.

The convoy stopped. I heard men speaking insistently. We all peeked out the slits along the side of the compartment and I could make out military men clustered around the doors of the first vehicle. Everyone was talking in the piercing, insistent tones this language produced when there was a dispute. It was not clear what was going on, but I noticed the soldiers in our APC with their hands tied had changed their expressions from fearful to wildly expectant. This must be good. They leaned forward and were listening. They sat up straighter and looked the guard in the eye in a friendly manner. It was as if they were regaining their manly demeanor, as groveling might no longer be required.

I looked to Tieng, but he ignored me as he listened intently.

The soldier guarding us looked pensive also. More men arrived and started ordering people about. They looked like higher-ranking men. Bags were brought out from the vehicles the new soldiers came in. Could it be? The commander of our column of vehicles was soon joined by other men who jumped down from the trucks and crowded around him. They all had very stern expressions. They opened the bags, suspiciously, and looked in, counting. I wondered if I was imagining this.

Heeding some unspoken impulse, Ganju and I simultaneously stood up, as if to exit the vehicle, but the guard shouted angrily and raised his gun at us. Another soldier on top of the vehicle peered in and banged the butt of his gun on the metal roof of the vehicle in warning. We sat back down.

Suddenly, it seemed that something was decided. Outside, a soldier shouted. Some of the new soldiers went into the first APC and took out a white tub of papers and dumped it into the canal along the road. Much of it soared off down the road and fluttered into the nearby rice fields. It was probably Thaw Kai's paperwork, mail, greeting cards drifting in the breeze, the detritus of the coup. I guess the soldiers wanted no part of this now. New drivers ran to the cabs of each of the APCs.

The column of vehicles made a U-turn and then turned north again on a road towards the city. Something's changed, I thought.

"We are going in another direction now. We are going to enter the city in a different zone," I said. Tieng looked skeptical. Ganju looked hopeful.

"Where are we going?" I said to our guard. He nodded nervously and made a sign to his men not to talk to us. The bound soldiers looked uncertain, but no longer terrified.

"You saw those bags?" Tieng said, under his breath. Yes, I nodded. They looked like the bags of money that had been in our control room.

Something was happening to divert our convoy from going directly to one of the prime minister's bases. Had we gone to a base under the control of the prime minister, it would have been disastrous. Where we were going now was unclear.

However, the closer we got to the city, the more relaxed it became. Our fellow prisoners with their hands tied relaxed and nodded to us as if all was okay. They cautiously chatted with the guard, but he still prevented us from exiting and would not let the soldiers untie their hands. He also refused to tell us where we were going or what was happening. It was maddening, more stressful than just knowing we were being delivered to Thaw Kai's clutches. I got the sense that both the maroon and brown-pinned soldiers had been bought off, but still insisted on custody of their prisoners. Then they could play both sides if they came back in contact with other military cliques.

Tieng remained hopeful. He said quietly, "They said, 'Comms are down.'"

I thought that Mike must have succeeded in his mission, at least—and that Thaw Kai's compound was not broadcasting.

I asked Tieng, "Where are we going?"

Tieng said, "I don't think it's to Thaw Kai's soldiers' barracks, but I'm not sure. We are still going to be in custody, probably."

"Do you think Chiang is sorting this out?" I said.

Tieng glared at me then glanced over to the other soldiers. I should not have said Chiang's name. Tieng said nothing more and folded his arms.

I looked at every watercourse, every dusty trail that ran away from the road for a way to escape. Each was a further last chance before we reached the unknown place we were being taken.

I could see Ganju was acutely aware of his surroundings, and, like me, was looking for an escape route. We were both the vast outsiders in this situation, completely disconnected from insight into what was really going on. I did not want to reach any destination with this collection of military men of ever-changing loyalties. Once they take down your name and get you to sign papers, you are in the system. Most other things one can run from, but getting in the system meant they got you.

I kept moving uncomfortably on the bench seat, looking back and forth to both sides of the road. Both Ganju and Tieng, I think, correctly interpreted that I was anxious for a chance to make a break for it. I would have to be sure I could struggle past our guard, who was seated by the only exit. As I was moving around restlessly in anticipation, Tieng covertly gestured to me, as if saying, "Don't." Tieng had already surprised me this day, so I took his warning seriously. Ganju had become still as a statue, like he was steeling himself for battle and was anxious to take action as well.

Our convoy entered the outskirts of the city, in the Chinatown area. Chinatown was part of every Asian capital holding the result of the waves of diaspora that emanated from China century after century. The convoy was going slower here. It had no choice, as small pedal-driven taxis constantly crisscrossed its path. Each one was pedaled by an elderly man, arms and legs merely sticks and sinew, pumping at the little bicycles with the same stupefied expressions on all of their faces.

The soldiers with us began whispering and then we heard yelling from others on the outside of the vehicle. I peeked through the slats at the front and could see a military blockade ahead. This caused great fear in all the soldiers. At the blockade, military men were waving national flags and holding up large placards showing the prime minister and the logo of his party. Several came down from the barricade and halted the convoy with rifles drawn.

I had to make an instant decision. I could see that these soldiers at the blockade were part of the prime minister's troops. However, these men were clearly stopping us— intercepting us and preventing an attempt to deliver the coup plotters to a neutral or friendly base. The blockade, so powerful in proclaiming allegiance to the prime minister, meant we were about to be delivered into the hands of Thaw Kai.

I saw no good way out. Guns were everywhere. I started to wish. "Come on!" I thought. Then my eyes were closed. "Come on. If you are there, help me out. Come on, Jesus, help me out." I was praying.

I was a person from a rich country, after all, skipping between the raindrops. I had been taught there was nothing beyond, that nothing meant anything, but I was praying. I thought I was smarter to dare more, but fate had brought me down and had made me pray. It was not really a big tragedy, but I had thought I could get away with not praying, with not begging into the void for help.

I looked over at Ganju, who was very slightly rocking, like he was amping himself up to make a move.

Not fearing anything now, I spoke out loud to him, not caring who heard.

"What do we do?"

He looked at me clearly and without fear. "The sword does not ask why it is sharp," he said.

Yeah, this is what I was made for. A conqueror. I know what I'm for. And I'll regret not being what I am. And I had come this far.

Maybe that was the answer to my prayer. Maybe that was my rationale for all that had happened and all that was to come.

I felt my bravado rising, as I knew that I was the only person who could save me. It was a rising elation. I looked back and forth from side to side of the APC, scanning for an escape route and not caring if the guard noticed this. I was tired of waiting. I raised myself out of my seat, clearly preparing to make a move, as I pushed through the crowded interior to the exit door. The soldier guarding us shouted and reached for me, but now was my chance. I violently pushed him back with all my effort, with one hand holding down the hand in which he held his gun. He fell back, something on his belt clanging loudly against the inside of the APC like a warning bell. His mustached face twisted up in anger as I held him off balance and struggled with the door handle, then flung the door open with a clank. I gave him a little nod of my head, an acknowledgement of my rudeness, before I sprang out the door. I expected to be grabbed from behind, but when I turned back, Ganju was there, right there, about to run over me, smiling fiercely. Tieng was jostling with someone in the background and then I saw him raise his big silver handgun from a rucksack with triumph. We all burst out of the APC, almost at once.

Some soldiers on top of the vehicles were shouting and aiming their rifles towards us, while most were occupied yelling back and forth at Thaw Kai's men at the blockade. It was a standoff, and this distraction worked in our favor.

I ran to an alley, daring them to shoot me in the back openly on the street, amid this chaos. This was the chance, my only chance.

Looking back for an instant, I saw Ganju and Tieng ducking around the outside of the APC to avoid the soldiers on top, both with rifles calmly aimed at me.

Ganju fled across the lanes of stopped traffic and into an opposite alley with Tieng following behind. Tieng was proudly flashing his gun. I wished I had been armed. That Thai was a better cowboy than I was.

I was already moving in the opposite direction from them down another alley. I was prepared for shots, ready to feel the singular experience of my flesh being torn by manmade objects too fast to see. But none were fired. Maybe I was right—they did not want to shoot me down in broad daylight.

I heard no one following, but kept moving, wanting to put distance between myself and whatever doom I was heading away from. I hoped the soldiers would remain occupied in the standoff at the blockade.

I did not stop moving, even when I was breathing heavily in the hot, thick air. With each step, I was elated again. I knew the secret back alleys, and even the ones I did not know, I figured I could find my way through.

I came to a massive market where produce and meat were laid out on beds of ice in all their bloody red and unhygienic glory. Other stalls displayed masses of oblong, spiral, and spiked local vegetables. Each person there who saw my stark white skin, my sweaty face, and my lanky frame ducking under the umbrellas of the market looked at me as if I were an alien being.

Then, crackling gun-fire echoed back from the street I had escaped from. It ripped through the still air, jolting everyone in the market. It meant that something bad was happening between the opposing soldiers back on the street. I had made the right decision to run, and I continued running.

5

Once shooting starts, right out on a street, there is little reason to decide between shooting a little or shooting a lot. Bullets are free to fly and be used as they were designed.

From the moment I first heard the crackle of gunfire, it seemed as though I would always hear the crackle of gunfire, sometimes near, sometimes far. It was now one with this place and I expected it. It was the reminder of uncertainty and the result of what we had unleashed.

I continued to move through the city. I passed shophouses—all plying their wares, open to the street. These usually had a TV inside the shop, switched on all the time. The family's grandmother, seated nearby, was forever looking to the street and then to the TV and back. As I passed, all such TVs showed the same image—the official military insignia. This was the sign of military action or civil unrest in these countries. Soon, a military man would come on all the channels and inform citizens that all was okay, and that the government was firmly in control—despite any evidence to the contrary.

Everywhere I went, each head turned to me. I wondered if news of the morning had alerted the citizens to the pernicious foreign influences that had tried to overthrow their government.

There was only one place to go to now—the safe house which was the annex. I recalled my experience with installing the new cone there and the apparent Western military men running the place. I thought the place must be a pseudo-embassy where we could regroup and find a way to get out of the country. With my passport stuck at the ministry, I was already imagining somehow getting to the border and crossing covertly to Thailand, as I heard this could be done, but it would be tricky, as the area was still controlled by rebels.

I got into a bicycle rickshaw. These were three-wheeled tricycle-like vehicles that plied the streets in Chinatown. They had canvas blinds that could be unfurled on each side and in front. This could obscure me from the outside world, as the old man, who was always the driver of such carts, pedaled his way across town to the annex. It was slow going and I felt sorry for these men who worked like this in the sun. The man's skin was the color of dark leather. He never stopped pedaling, working harder at it than I ever could.

I finally arrived at the annex. Gunfire, remote or near, it was hard to tell, rang out occasionally. I found the ground floor of the annex empty—a reception desk and furnishings waiting for a normal workday. I heard voices upstairs and ascended the stairs.

The upstairs stairway opened onto a large area with windows to the front and back and hallways that led to suites of rooms at either end of the building. People were hurrying about, mostly imported Thais from CLB. All had frantic looks on their faces. Some carried packed suitcases or were clutching paperwork as they assembled in a hopeful line, ready for imminent departure. There was no sign of any Western military men—they had cleared out. All were locals and Thais.

Some soldiers thundered up the stairs behind me. They were our white-pinned soldiers, all with weapons at the ready and worried faces. It was not a comforting sight.

Tieng was there. He greeted me with a tip of the head from across the room, as if nothing had happened. Maybe like me, he was elated by the challenge and the chance we had taken. He was standing as if ready to spring into battle, with his flashy silver handgun holstered on his hip. His lovely girlfriend was beside him, similarly armed and alert.

Amnuay was speaking to them. He had made it here too. It looked like he was giving them orders.

He was composed, the boss of the company, and was organizing people and telling some to stop yelling and be quiet. He noticed me and looked me up and down. I realized the entire front of my clothing was covered in mud, as if I had fallen on the ground. I could not recall falling, but the mud proved I had, and with circumstances so pressing in my escape, my mind had just ignored this and urged me on. He looked as if he were surprised to see me. He paused, looking at me like he was planning something. Then he said solemnly, "Come with me. Someone wants to speak with you."

He led me into a room. This was the same room in which I had been mistaken for John and told about the cones used to irradiate people. The metal panels on the walls and ceiling gave it an air of a special, expectant place. The periodic gunfire outside was muffled to gentle thuds in here. I brushed the drying mud off my clothes.

Amnuay picked up a phone and dialed. After a moment, he handed it to me. Chiang was on the line. And he was furious. He said I was finished. I tried to explain that, when we got to the compound, Thaw Kai was already gone, and by the time we left his house, the other soldiers had surrounded us. That is what I intended to say, but I heard it coming out like a babbling excuse. I should have argued something like, "It wasn't my fault that the intelligence was bad," and "The communications array was not accessible from the residence."

But he stopped me and in a very Thai way said, "Let me finish." This meant he was going to make a speech. There was quite a lot about "You should have known" and "You should have been more careful with what you said." I did not understand why I was being blamed for this, as what had happened was completely out of my hands. I was only carrying a backpack of radios.

It is disheartening and infuriating when the person you desire to impress becomes disenchanted with you. I did not even think to say, "What is going to happen to us now?" I was not sure whether I was crestfallen or angry. Chiang sat in his luxurious overseas estate while I was doing the dirty work. I had taken a chance. I guess it was clear I could have no business relationship with this barbarian. He probably thought the same about me. There would be no schools, no lucrative contracts for me, no future with Rangsei. It had slipped away. It was that easy.

He ended the conversation politely, but curtly, saying goodbye, and I servilely said goodbye as well. There was no use arguing. I was sure Amnuay was blaming me. He had Chiang's ear. I could not win. Chiang's anger was the least of my problems now, and I did not want to push back against the only person who might be still pulling strings to rescue us all.

I exited the room, and a rat-a-tat-tat of shots rang out at the front of the building, then more crackles of gunfire from undetermined locations. Everyone ducked for cover, but I stood there like a dumb foreigner, thinking that I was above the fray and how absurd it was. Then the windows on the front side shattered as bullets with cartoony sounding zips shot into the room and impacted the ceiling, sending out a compact explosion of cement shards where they hit. This was serious. I knew this was not a place I should have come to.

And I realized Mike was nowhere to be found. And Don and John were too smart to be here.

People began to crawl around, repositioning themselves. More blips of gunfire erupted, then yelling on both sides, the white-pin soldiers shouting to whoever was shooting outside. It was local idiomatic speech to tell someone to calm down— "Hey, hey, hey"—speech that people say to others to bring them to reality when their tempers are out of control.

Sounds of shooting then came from the floor below in the reception area. The sound came up the stairs, echoing off the hard cement of the building's walls and ceiling and creating a discomforting ring. I wanted to think we were fighting back and that an airplane was being prepared for evacuation, but it did not seem likely. The sensations of the day were combining to shake my confidence. It was a physical rattling, ears ringing and air full of dust and a smell of burning. Then there was another tangle of noise, an exchange of gunfire with impacts cracking off buildings or vehicles outside. Then a pause, then more "Hey, hey, hey" being exchanged as rival soldiers attempted to calm the situation.

Then an abrupt silence. After a moment, downstairs, there was another shattering din of shooting back and forth. Each barrage ended with a whiny bell-like ring as the sounds passed through the building, and my ears rang painfully. A sound so complete, overriding all sensation, that I imagined that all soldiers in war must end up deaf. It was a breathtaking sound, so great that it must mean that death was upon us.

Then an avalanche of our white-pin soldiers came up the stairs, running in panic, emerging out of dust and smoke, stumbling over each other, throwing down their guns. They were hotly followed by another group bounding up the stairs. They were brown-pin soldiers, firing mainly into the ceiling, and everyone was shouting, "Hey, hey, hey" at each other.

People moved in every direction, crashing and falling over. Under fire, people moved with alarming speed. I escaped down one of the halls and into one of the rooms. Someone was behind me. It was Phong.

He was now a fully competent soldier standing correctly as a sensible human with proper uniform and proud brown unit pin of the prime minister's troops.

So, he had been a plant, playing a fool, not only for me, but for everyone at CLB and the friendly base. I wondered why Mike had been so sure of his loyalty. Now Phong was doing his duty, proudly, with his rifle leveled at me a few meters away. He then shot directly at me.

It was such a singular cacophonous sound in that square cement room, greater than anything I had heard before, that the sound itself made me think I had been hit.

By whatever providence or dumb luck of a young man, the bullet did not hit me. However, I sensed it whiz past my right ear and then my ear was ringing, and I was hit in the face with a handful of grit and dust. The angle of the rifle and the geometry of the shot must have conspired to save me from consequence, or else it was magic, and my red amulet was doing its duty.

I knew then that I was special, superior maybe. He had aimed directly at me, and the bullet decided to miss. And I understood why he had shot at me. It was clear, crystallizing in the moment, that I was nothing other than destiny, aggressive destiny, and one cannot take chances with that.

I lunged forward towards the barrel of his rifle and yanked it up into the air. It might have been hot, but I did not feel it. I went towards him with full force. Yeah, this is how I imagine Ganju would do it.

Phong was clearly surprised I was not shot and then surprised I was upon him in an instant. We grappled as more shots crackled from outside the room in the hall.

Phong was a wily fighter, but I got my arm around his neck as his hands tried to draw down the gun which I had pushed up. He reached for a sheathed knife on his hip, which I barely managed to slap away. Then he went back to the gun and my free hand flailed against his, and his other hand's fingernails ground into my arm that was around his neck. But I would not relent. I was slowly choking him. He would not stop writhing, and I could not get the gun out of his hand, and I did not want him to call out for others to come to his aid, not knowing which side would come. That is my excuse. I held on with all my might.

Then, I think, right there, he died, not with a manly gunshot, but with a quiet suffocation.

I drew my hands back and he slumped forward to the floor. He was completely still. I thought that I should do CPR, but I took a step back. Whether he lived or died would be up to his fate. I would not intervene. My obligation to him, to anything, was at an end.

I ruefully thought that it should have been a cowboy confrontation on a ruined street. Something honorable. Fighting a worthy opponent, not this dreck. But this was a different time and a different place. Real life was a terrible mess.

Then, almost involuntarily, I thought that I never wanted to be in a situation where I would have to kill someone again. This thought was completely logical, at least for my sanity, but thinking it surprised me.

I wanted to say something, make a statement, but I looked down at him and all that came out was "Okay." The thing that had happened was the only thing that could have happened, I told myself.

I realized that the hallway was quiet, but then more shots rang out. Then lots more of the "Hey, hey, hey." I somehow hated hearing that more than the shooting itself—the plaintive voices of men on different sides calling out to each other.

I ventured into the hall. Tieng was shielding himself behind a supporting column of the building, silver gun in hand, towering over the others who were still cowering. Shards of cement littered the floor, and a burning smell crowded into the building like many firecrackers. The power had been cut at some point—I did not notice when—and it was now dark in the hall, with bold shafts of bright light coming through the windows. It was bright afternoon light now, and the bright parts of the building were terribly bright, and the dark parts were ghastly black. A long smear of blood was on the floor, as if someone had been shot and dragged away. Nearby, two of our white-pin soldiers were wounded. One was sitting up. The other was lying flat, still conscious. Others were attending to them, some calm, some crying in fear.

Tieng looked over to me and said to me directly and confidently, "I bought us some time. I gave them one of the bags that was kept in reserve." His eyes were steely. He meant he had given the soldiers one of the remaining bags of money in return for their retreat. Where it had come from, I did not know, but he had taken charge. His eyebrows were raised, and his voice rang out as if he had been hit with an electric shock, precisely the shock men feel when they are exposed to sudden battle, leaving them in an otherworldly and elated state.

A man looked out of a room on the other side of the hall and said something in Thai. I knew what he said. It was,

"Someone has died." I went into the room. Others were hovering over a man's body on the floor. It was lying flat.

"What happened?" a voice said. On the floor the man's shirt was ripped open and someone listened to his chest to hear a heartbeat. I saw no wounds.

The man looked like a totally inanimate piece of wood, like something that could never have been alive. It was Amnuay, now gone. I wondered if he had a hidden bullet hole somewhere. Someone said, "Heart attack."

How weird to have dodged the bullets and then have one's own body kill itself.

Despite the chaos of the last few minutes, this sudden pause elicited a moment of emotion. It made me think of the comforting Caucasian Jesus who forever looked down on me as a child. It had come to this again.

It occurred to me then that I had not seen Ganju. He was a warrior, and smarter than I was, refusing to be trapped here.

I knew I had to get out now. This was not ending well. I would not be trapped. I still thought I was above it all. There was always a chance. Thinking this was probably a trick of my mind that would save me.

I moved to the front side of the building facing the street. I sidled up to the window from one wall, standing erect, edging my head out to look outside. There were lots of soldiers, more trucks arriving and soldiers jumping out of them.

A man on a bullhorn began shouting. It appeared that, within a few minutes, the soldiers would coalesce, their resolve bolstered by the new men arriving, and a final attempt would be made to capture the building and its occupants.

Since the coup was a bust, they would be striking back hard. Prime Minister Thaw Kai would use this singular time to settle scores—even those unrelated to the coup. Those who had grudges could make their move to murder and others might find their shops burned by rivals. Chaos was expected. It was a window to be taken advantage of by the crafty man, and then typically forgiven in a post-coup amnesty to ensure a return to a harmonious society. It was the rare time one could go about shooting and burning down the houses of one's enemies.

Soldiers were already exiting the building below me from the bottom floor with hands raised. I could not possibly surrender now. I had traipsed through the prime minister's house. I had killed people. I had killed people with my bare hands. Every white-pin soldier could be ordered to testify against me. Everyone would think the worst and they would not be wrong.

With my ears still ringing, I attempted to create a meditative silence within my head and quiet my fretful thoughts. Whatever was going to happen, I was not going to have my last stand be here in this crummy building.

I looked out a back window. Most often there was no rear exit out of such buildings, as compounds were surrounded by high walls topped with barbed wire or broken glass or both, like the CLB compound. When I looked out, I saw that this place was no different.

I went down the hall, past the room Phong was in. I tried not to look in but could not help it. He was still there; apparently no one had found him yet. Others were standing here and there, talking in hushed tones, some weeping, and outside, the bullhorn address was still going on in the local tongue.

At the end of the hall was another open stairway. I walked down cautiously to the first floor. It was deserted and calm. I went to one of the back rooms—a kitchen. This was common in office buildings, as sometimes janitorial staff, always older jovial females, would cook food for the staff. Right outside of the kitchen was the lean-to and the small open area where pans would be washed and then dried in the sun. It was a space only a meter between the back of the building and the high wall bounding the site.

There was no gate through the back wall, as expected. The wall itself was dauntingly high and was topped with bundles of barbed wire. I went back into the kitchen and looked around for some inspiration. I went into one of the side rooms by the kitchen where cleaning supplies were stored. Even places like this the locals made homey, sometimes sleeping on the job, or listening to the radio after hours. That meant there must be a mattress-like bed roll for naps, and, next to the cleaning supplies, I did find a thin bed mat. I grabbed it and threw the unrolled mattress over the barbed wire. I found the old plastic chair that was always in such a place to sit on while washing the dishes. I stood on the chair and grabbed onto the mat. It was firmly snagged on the barbed wire. I carefully climbed up the mat until I was astride the barbed wire. I could hardly believe I was doing this. I was escaping. However, with each movement, tearing sounds came from the mat as it pulled against the barbed wire. I threw my other leg over and roughly slid down the other side of the wall. I came down hard and lost my footing as I fell to the ground. When I looked up, standing there, flat against the wall, was a single soldier with a rifle slung over his shoulder.

He was chewing something. It was probably betel nut that people chewed as a mild narcotic stimulant. He looked mildly surprised, and my heart sank as I steeled myself for a new fight. But my sudden appearance must have been a surprise that petrified him—a pale whiteface falling from above. I had no idea how long the pause would last, so I jumped to my feet, turned my back to him confidently and walked off. Maybe he had never seen a creature like me. He made no sign to me and I was getting away. It was a lucky break. I was losing the heart to fight again this day anyway.

6

Military trucks were on every road as I walked along. I imagined that loyal troops from countryside bases would be pouring into the city, told that communists or some other unredeemable foe was menacing their nation. Extermination would be the only logical way to save the land.

The smeared blood and gun shots of the annex were hanging in my mind. Had we not been so lackadaisical... Had we not neglected to properly reconnoiter the Lion's Den beforehand... Had the plan not been talked about by so many people...

I needed a way out and that meant regaining my passport. I knew there were consular services for the U.S. and European countries set up in a hotel, but I could not recall which one and I did not want to go around town searching for a place I was not sure of while the government and military were fighting among themselves and probably looking for me.

I headed back to the area I knew, near the CLB complex. I exited the pedal taxi a couple blocks away.

I paid the driver more than he asked so he would be happy, but not enough that he might brag to his friends that a rich foreigner had overpaid him, maybe bringing my presence to attention.

I entered a shophouse with an open-air front within sight of CLB so I could see what was going on surreptitiously. I had been to this place to buy snacks before.

Pretending to examine the bread, I casually glanced down the street to the CLB. Military trucks were in front. Army men stood there, not casually wandering about, but observant and serious, holding guns and looking ready.

The city always had a din—construction banging and belching trucks struggling through the potholed side streets— but it was all quiet now except for the occasional rat-a-tat-tat of gunfire in the distance that was growing closer.

Don and John were being led out of the gates of the CLB. They were gesturing and talking in an animated fashion with the soldiers. John held a book, a bilingual dictionary, and was pointing to it, trying to make himself understood. The soldiers were guiding them onto a military truck. The conversation was still friendly, but I could see, even from across the street, that Don and John were trying to avoid getting into the truck. I wondered how they managed to get caught after all. I never heard what happened to them.

There was no going back there. The company was finished—particularly for me. If I could only get out of the country, I could relax again. If not, I was sure it would be unpleasant. There is a thin divide between doom and having a good story to tell.

I exited the shop and turned the corner. Then I felt a big flat hand on my shoulder. As always, it was Mike.

He was dressed head to foot in a U.S. sailor's uniform and sat astride his tiny 2-stroke Honda motorcycle. His uniform was sparkling white with bell-bottom pants legs and black shoes and a jaunty sailor's hat like Popeye's. On this giant of a man, in this blazing afternoon sun, it was as startling and conspicuous an outfit as could be worn. And yet, he was too slippery to be caught at the annex as I had been.

"They tricked us," he said. "Thaw Kai's men just pretended to run away. Once you entered the Lion's Den they circled back. Glad you got out."

"Yeah, I had to run for my life," I said. To me, it was like saying, "I had to pray."

He revved his motorcycle as if warning he would soon be on his way. He went on conspiratorially,

"You know, Thaw Kai was hiding right there out of sight the whole time in his house, and the word is that the whole communications array was rigged to blow up anyway. You're braver than I!" He laughed.

I had been lucky again. Or unlucky. At this point I did not know.

"You were successful, at least," I said.

"Had some luck there. The yahoos knocked it out. Probably more dependable than soldiers," he said.

"So CLB is finished?"

"Thaw Kai, he outfoxed us, made Chiang lose," he said. "There'll be no CLB here now, gotta get out. Someone talked."

Mike let the motorcycle rev down to a purr. He leaned forward a bit to me.

"Girl got to you?" he said. He said it sincerely, like a friend who knows another friend is a fool.

"What?" Then I knew. Somehow, he knew about Rangsei. And this was what Chiang had been referring to on his phone call to me at the annex.

I was suddenly as astonished as if I had been shot myself, my mouth open in surprise.

"No, no, nobody knew anything. She knew nothing." I stammered out my reply. "I didn't say anything."

"Okay," Mike said.

At another time, I might have protested more vigorously, angrily denying it, but now I was wise enough to know this would have made me appear more guilty. They would just believe what they would believe—as would I.

"Gotta get out of this country now, you know?" he said. A shudder of gunfire erupted, now much closer. "It's a free-for-all," he added.

"I need my passport," I said, almost pitifully.

"Can't help you there. You'll need a miracle. A white boy's miracle." He laughed in a way that made me realize the absurdity of my predicament.

I began to speak, a plea for help, but he gave me no further chance to speak. He gave me a friendly mock salute, and rode off.

He circled to the other side of the street by the military trucks at the gates of the CLB with a huge smile on his face, as if showing he had all the luck and all the gall in the world.

I should have been angry, being abandoned by Mike, but he somehow gave me confidence, even as he was leaving me to fend for myself.

I was starting to feel that I did not need his help or anyone else's. I would find a way, my own way, like I always did, as a strange person doing impossible things so far away from home. Maybe I would walk to the border, past the rebels, past the mines. If I were bold like Mike, things would come together in my favor, and this day was far from over.

7

I took the series of back alleys to my apartment, my secret back alleys. I heard the rat-a-tat-tat moving toward me again. I thought I could sense people becoming scared and moving more quickly to return to the safety of their homes. The rat-a-tat-tat was growing more insistent.

At the front entrance of my apartment were several muscular local soldiers who I had never seen before. I could not see their unit pins and thus did not know which side they were on, if that even mattered anymore. They stood in the sun, peering up and down the street, as if they had just arrived and were looking for something. Then they ducked inside the building.

They were waiting for me, I was sure. I surveyed this scene from a shophouse across the street. Everything in the shop was brought in from neighboring Thailand—potato chips, packages of doughy bread infused with sugary goo, and Fanta sodas in all their lurid colors. All junk. I pretended that I was pondering the purchase of a sack of potato chips as I calculated what to do.

I began to feel a strange resignation to my fate, a calmness in direct opposition to the reality. It made me chuckle at my predicament. Like I was free even when I was trapped. But this passed, as more gunfire erupted in the distance. I had pushed too far and messed everything up.

Mike's words, "It's a free-for-all," hung in my mind. This is what I had dreamed about—the chaos and fall of a capital, but I was failing with nowhere to hide, not even a loyal girlfriend to help me. Who could possibly help me now? I needed a miracle, and I knew I should not have imagined it would come from a woman.

Then I heard her.

It was a voice with a certain grating, persistent tone. Some females had that voice, and it just carried. It was Noi. I could not hear what she was saying, but it was her. She was complaining loudly to the soldiers there and pushing past them as she exited the front of my apartment building. The soldiers watched her, scowling. She turned down the sidewalk like a soldier herself and began to emphatically walk back in the direction of the CLB.

Making sure I was not noticed, I moved out of the shop, patting the cat that was sleeping on the bread. I walked along, parallel to Noi on the other side of the street. Once fully out of sight of my apartment, I crossed over the street to her.

"Noi," I said.

"Oh, it's you." She spoke distractedly as if she had expected me to arrive and I was late again. She did not look at me, but immediately started rummaging through her large carry-all bag. It was full of paperwork. She flipped through some plastic folders and in one was a manila envelope with my name, "Bert Mars," on it. She handed the envelope to me.

I held it and instantly knew what it must contain. It was my passport. I looked in and there it was. Everything was legal. With a stern frown on her face, she handed me a receipt to sign. I signed it "Mickey Mouse," as I typically signed official paperwork no one checked. It was my own tiny defiance. She put the receipt away without looking at it.

"The ministry works half-days on Saturday. They finished this morning. I thought you might want it, so I was going to give it to you on the way back to the office."

It was incredibly considerate of her. I was overjoyed. I felt like hugging her.

"Better not go back to the office," I told her.

"Don't you think I know that?" she said to me, like I was insultingly stupid. "They would not let me in this morning. It's a bunch of bullshit." She said the word "bullshit" in a hushed tone in the way my mother once did, as if she were cursing and simultaneously blaming me for making her curse.

"I'm going back and just stand there until they let me in," she said. I believed her.

I found myself grinning uncontrollably. "Thanks for bringing me back my passport. I really appreciate it."

This is what she was looking for—praise for her actions. She said, "You're welcome," suddenly pleased with me. "I have to get to work now," she said, returning to her businesslike demeanor. Her shoes clicked as she walked off, conspicuously a little faster than everyone else on the street, as if to demonstrate the importance of the tasks she had to attend to.

I now possessed my passport. I knew I had the boon of unknowable luck in the freebooting tropics. There was now no good reason to consider anything before this moment. No reason to ever go back to old dreams.

I turned my thoughts to my tiny apartment with its basic accouterments—toothbrush, clothes, books, some newspapers, and the cheap suitcase I arrived with, the ice-cold shower and cheap furniture.

She was probably there, waiting for me. I'll come back; I promise. I involuntarily imagined saying this to her. So sad a young man could think of saying this to a clear betrayer. I thought of saying it again, but with sarcasm, as I held my passport tightly.

But I could still be caught in this web. I knew too many things. The whole plot. The cones that we used to kill our enemies. I was in the pay of Chiang. I had been in Thaw Kai's house during the coup. People had died around me. Being such a bad liar, I would surely crack if I were caught. It was time to go.

8

I hailed a taxi and told the driver, "Airport." The moment I got in, the door on the other side of the taxi sprang open and Rangsei got in as well. My mouth opened in shock to tell the taxi to stop, but the driver had already pulled away and we were careening through traffic.

Rangsei said, "I was looking for you. I followed you from your apartment." She had been waiting for me, as I'd suspected. She looked down, almost ashamed, then looked back up to me.

"You don't have a chance. The prime minister knows how to handle things. He... he controls everything." She was dropping any pretense. I tried to resist her and imagined the words, "You'll get a fair trial" being part of what she said.

"Come with me now," she said. "Be honest with yourself." There were tears in her eyes.

"No way," I thought, but said nothing.

"We can still be together," she pleaded.

People were hurrying home on bicycles. Many shops, normally open, were already closed for the day. Gunfire sputtered in the distance. I gestured to all this outside, playing dumb, and said, "What's this about?" We nearly both laughed at the same time. As we often did. We both knew.

I turned to her and said kindly, "The fortune teller. That was too much."

She bristled just a bit.

"What did you expect to find?" I continued. I still wanted to throw her off the scent. "Watching over me?"

An angry look crept over her face.

"This is my country, not yours," she said. "And then the Thai tycoons come here. It's all for sale... or stolen or about to be. Right?"

I was not in the right about anything, I realized, but before I could think up a reply, she continued.

"You have to come with me now." She spoke like a police officer. "You have nowhere to go."

I let myself smirk at her then.

"I'm not going with you," I said. "I'm not the kind who gets caught."

"I'm not going to leave you, Bert," she said, moving closer to me and taking hold of my arm. "I'm not giving up on you."

"Still playing the game?" I said.

Her face softened. "I am sincere. You should know that," she replied.

I knew everything about her and all that was going on, but I felt the pull of my old dreams. But I was too clever to be tricked by my own human desire. I noticed her tousled hair for the last time and turned slightly away from her. It was a blind that went down, never to rise again.

"I'm pregnant," she said. It was said inartfully and quickly, as if a last chance to get me to give myself up peacefully. She took out a paper from her pocket and carefully unfolded it to show me. Something about a pregnancy. I thought maybe she was indeed sincere, but by now I could not really tell anymore. I glanced over but refused to look at it further.

The taxi was making good time. Soon it would be apparent that I was headed to the airport. If my luck was holding, she was assuming that my passport was out of reach at the ministry. I had suspected the ministry knew about the plot, but maybe they knew nothing and that is why I had my passport now. There was no way to know how fortune had favored me. My head was spinning thinking of it. She must not know I was making my escape. But I feared she could start calling out for the police at any moment.

The taxi was waiting at an intersection, one of several to pass through before getting to the airport road.

The back seats of these taxis where we sat had been reupholstered into broad, flat bench seats. I reached across her. There was a momentary spark of surprise, perhaps delight in her eyes, as she thought I was going to embrace her. I flung open the door and kicked her out of the car. She slid easily across the seat and then her feet hooked the bottom edge of the door frame, and she tumbled out.

She thudded to the ground with surprising roughness. I winced, only then admitting that this was all going away for good.

I pulled the door shut while shouting to the driver, "Go, go!" The driver knew what "Go" meant. He chuckled as we sped off. He was probably thinking, "Lover's quarrel." It was something that would always be. It made me know all the drama of life was forever close—the beginning and end, the shouting and the stillness of her voice, the not knowing we ever were.

She was getting up as we pulled away. I had surprised her and probably knocked the wind out of her. She had a despairing look on her face that pained me. I hoped she would be okay. I did not want to hurt anyone anymore. I wished she had never existed, and I had never existed. It was interesting to acknowledge that love was the only thing, while at the same time throwing it all away.

I was my own mistake and the mistake of the whole world—those who dared to go out, those who wanted to do anything but what they were expected to do, and those who could never go back.

9

As I moved out of the city and towards the airport, I could see the rising panic. A few pedicabs were abandoned in the street and most shophouses already had pulled down their metal security blinds. The small makeshift markets on every other corner were closing too, and pickups were being hastily loaded up by panicked vendors.

Military men in trucks were everywhere. Young men on their motorcycles, who normally rode with a fearless gusto, now rode even more recklessly, traveling in both directions on both sides of the road. The traffic slowed and some vehicles awkwardly turned around on the busy road, heading back towards us, going the wrong way.

"No, no. Think closed," the taxi driver said, meaning that the airport was shut down, but I had no choice and urged him on.

I was worried that the taxi would be stopped, but the relative chaos reassured me. Surely this meant that order and control had not yet been reestablished. Maybe I could still get away.

We were halted at a military checkpoint on the final stretch of the long straight road to the airport entrance. At the roadside, soldiers were being held at gunpoint by other soldiers, kneeling with their hands on their heads. The soldiers manning the checkpoint spoke to the taxi driver offhandedly as if the entire affair on this Saturday evening was a common annoyance. One of the soldiers looked closely at me. He gestured at me to get out. I pretended not to understand. I did not want to get out, only to go on.

The soldier then talked to the taxi driver and then to no one in particular, I think. He was a broad-faced man, young, but already wise-looking.

He poked his head into the car and looked me up and down closely. Then he drew back and in came his wide farmer's hand. It touched the gold metal chain around my neck and then moved down to rest on my amulet—the tiny red Buddha. The angular shape of the amulet on its chain was clearly visible through my shirt. I drew it out and showed it to him, dangling it on its chain.

I wondered if he was wanting it as a bribe. I took the necklace off and handed it to him.

He held the amulet in his hand—in a gruff way, shook it a bit, quite rudely, but as he did, his expression changed and he looked at me with a surprising sympathy, almost as if he felt sorry for me.

His expression not changing, he gently put the amulet back into my hand. Perhaps he was remembering something, perhaps it had made him sympathize with me, a clueless foreigner frightened by his strange and violent land. I will never know. He waved us on.

At the airport, the vast white wall of the building was already pockmarked with bullet holes and the fragments of the concrete lay on the pavement below.

We came to a stop. I paid the driver, and he grunted, expressionless. Then he smiled like he was reassuring me and saying, "I've seen it all."

The airport was frantic and loud. Agitated voices echoed off the ceiling. To my relief, I was easily able to buy a ticket to Bangkok. I asked if the airport had been closed for a time due to the shooting outside. The attendant said with her best forced smile, "Now it is open!" Good customer service was only giving good news.

Shooting stuttered in the near distance, causing everyone in the terminal to pause and go silent. Then some local men in Western suits came out from a back room. They looked like managers. They waved their hands at the passengers as if they were going to make an announcement, but only said "Okay, okay!" They looked panicked themselves.

I stood in line at immigration, wondering if my name was on a list to be detained. I was trembling, my ears began to ring, and I thought I could smell gunpowder again. Like immigration officers in most countries, the one checking my passport did not look at me. He was surely sick of all these foreigners, as all immigration officers were, and just wanted to go home on time. He only briefly flipped open my passport. It must be a grueling job. I did notice that for the other Westerners departing that day, the officers also waved them quickly through immigration. Perhaps the officers were a bit embarrassed that their country had scared them. I was stamped out and passed through customs.

"I've still got it," I thought. The old feeling of elation was returning. I had taken a chance and made it so far.

Then there he was, Thaw Kai, on all of the monitors in the departure area. His hectoring teeth. He looked like a furious and determined man trying to remain calm. He was a farmer who had somehow climbed atop all of his kinsmen, and he was going to stay there. I had looked into his eyes and shaken his hand. I had his hairbrush in my pocket still.

So far, I was nearly through this ordeal without real terror, without regret. I was saving all that for later. Had to get away first. Sitting on the plastic airport seats, waiting for the plane's gears to be oiled and baggage loaded and planes to be towed and moved, I was again powerless.

The shops in the departure area were selling duty-free alcohol and cigarettes and perfume. Travelers were serenely looking for bargains as if this were a day like any other. I could now clearly hear shooting—pops—nearby.

I hoped whoever was getting shot was getting what they deserved. But I was smart enough to get away. I smirked to myself. Then I started to feel dizzy. My head felt like it was soaring out of my body, and then I had that most common and visceral desire of a living creature—the need to vomit. Vomiting was teaching me what I was—base, better days behind, destined to cease and decay.

But I resisted; I would not faint or vomit. I looked out across the flat, angular tarmac, telling myself that what endured was nothing from the dreaded spume of the body, but instead some tale of challenge, and then triumph, or at least the ability to endure. Even my failures would be slowly repurposed by the deep hidden ego into learning experiences, stoicism, or admirable legend.

So, this is what I was, maybe what this place was, a string of the visceral—vomit, anger, failures, fainting, violence—that is subtly repurposed into legend and history.

My flight number appeared at the gate. People stood in anticipation. I suddenly felt fine. I was now in a line, then walking across the tarmac, then ever so slowly making my way up the stairs to the plane. Other foreigners were lugging huge carry-on bags, spiriting their precious possessions out of the country. I carried nothing other than my passport.

Once on board, my mood dimmed and I thought that any minute the plane would be boarded, and I would be dragged off. But the plane was pushed back and started to move away. I slowly began to smirk, then smile like a maniac, probably. I could not help it. I was getting away. Then we taxied down the runway, then rolled and rolled, and then finally lifted into the air. Was this really happening? Might we be called back? "Let me get away," I said to the clouds. This was the space between disaster and an epic story to tell.

Later, I found that my plane was among the last— perhaps the very last—that left before gunfire again closed the airport.

It should have all gone badly. They could have gotten me in some third world court and made me play the bad guy. I would have to feign shock and surprise over and over in court until I became that resigned, sullen-faced foreign prisoner that I always saw in the press, one that had given up all protestations of indignation, knowing he was caught. The locals would chuckle that this poor foreigner must not have enough influence and money to get off, or maybe he foolishly thought that justice would always prevail, and he would be treated with deference. Oh, how they would have chuckled at me, but here I was, in a plane arcing away, its machinery roaring as it does after takeoff, as if to demonstrate it was getting free of the hot ground and escaping into the freedom of the atmosphere.

PART VI

1

Once back in Bangkok, I read the news. No mention of the chaos or the shooting from where I had fled from, but there were murky rumors of a possible coup.

Within the week, news trickled out of a failed, bloodless coup. It was also reported that a businessman, Amnuay, died at his home in Bangkok. I decided to believe all of it. It would have been nice to acknowledge what happened so each of us would be remembered for the lives we led and the deaths we died and the real reasons for it, so that the people who were still alive could really live, but it was hard to accept it had turned so dirty and complicated.

From my perspective, it was all about Chiang and Thaw Kai, but in the years afterwards, reading about the events, it was clear I was involved in only one aspect of the overall disgruntlement with the regime.

Before the coup, many military and business leaders had been subtly queried on their feelings about their prime minister. Then, egged on by the growing cadre of those who felt wronged by Thaw Kai and those who imagined climbing the ladder of power that was monopolized by Thaw Kai and his allies, an impetus for a change arose.

Other parts of the rebellion came from opposition parties, each of which had their own loyal military cliques. Thaw Kai had a lot of enemies, but he ended up beating them all. It will go on, I guess. Nothing ended. The dictators and billionaires are still dictators and billionaires.

Several "Thai businessmen," likely meaning Thai employees of CLB, were rounded up and imprisoned. Later, Thais from a wide range of companies got caught up in the dragnet, even though they had no connection to the event. All were soon released, but by the end of the year, several Thai businesses had their long concessions cancelled, including one from a fledging airline, but I never knew if these other companies were actually involved in the plot.

That Monday, I returned to the CLB headquarters in Bangkok like nothing had happened. To my shock and amazement, Noi was right there at her desk arranging paperwork while sharply commanding one of the cleaning ladies. She looked up at me with astonishment, I guess assuming I had vanished into Thaw Kai's prison, but this was only for a moment. She composed her face into her best office day dullness and nodded as I passed by.

I walked back through the building into what used to be the technical area where I worked. Everything there was completely reorganized. There were now cubicles full of marketing people on the phone talking to potential advertisers. I asked around, but no one knew anything about my old department.

One part of me planned to find my old chair in the office and go about working as normal. I had a burning desire to know I was still employed by the company, despite all that had happened.

I made a circuit of the offices and then ended up back where Noi was seated.

I asked her, "How am I going to get paid?" By this, I meant my last paycheck from CLB International from the other country.

She put on that smile that Thais use when they are extremely uncomfortable. Foreigners, who do not know better, mistake it for a friendliness, but, no, it is a smile of horror.

"I will find out," she said. I took another circuit of the office to see if I could locate anyone I remembered, but everybody was new. The turnover in these places was great. It was a well-known characteristic of young Thai workers that they would switch over to a new job for the smallest increase in pay, even if it meant they had to take the bus for three more hours across town each day.

No one knew anything about Tieng either. I imagine he was somewhere, meekly sorting out the mysteries of equipment in a darkened control room, all the while ready to put on his silver handgun and take charge.

I came back to Noi's desk. She held her head aloft, and, almost regally, said, "You work for that company. You will have to talk to them." Then she added, before I could protest, "And that company has ceased operations."

"Well, what about you?" I said. I did not quite want to ask if I was still employed at CLB in Bangkok in case I would be told "No." I imagined Noi would love to tell me that.

"You can talk to the MD," she said, and picked up the phone.

I sat down to ponder. I did not want to beg, but I needed a work permit and visa to work and be able to stay in paradise.

Some Thais arrived, one older, concerned-looking man, I guess the managing director, and two women carrying paperwork. They did not introduce themselves and I could feel they wanted nothing to do with me. The man tilted his head as if in kindness and told me I was no longer an employee of CLB Thailand and I would have to leave.

I could see he was preparing himself for a big noisy argument and protest from me, probably a protest demanding my rights. This is what Thais expected from Westerners, who they stereotyped, perhaps quite correctly, as loud, opinionated, and disagreeable. I could see the man holding his breath and getting ready to parry the arguments and flailing arms of an agitated foreigner.

However, the air had gone out of me. My appetite for a fight was gone, left behind in that place where I had almost made my fortune and lost the girl. I simply let them show me the door. They left me on the front sidewalk. The man was enormously relieved, and I was strangely happy not to have upset him.

2

I tried various ways to contact Chiang, attempting to ingratiate myself with him again, but he was now forever beyond my reach. He went on to greater heights of politics as well as the depths of defeat before rebounding. That made me all the more rueful that I was blamed for the failure of our bold endeavor and left behind. Life is eventually just pondering what other paths one could have taken. I can only imagine where I could have ended up if I had stayed in his good graces, if I had succeeded.

I did sometimes think that they would come for me to eliminate the evidence and my testimony, but they did something worse—they ignored me.

Maybe I was not the real cause of the failure of the plot—maybe I was a scapegoat—but I imagined that it suited everyone to say that I was a lightweight and consign me to the oblivion of the life of a schoolteacher. I had tried to start a legend, but it just turned out to be dirty rumors. Maybe they thought, perhaps quite rightly, that no one would believe my story if they heard it.

I went crawling back to my old salaried job at the school—my Stockholm syndrome.

To my relief, I was welcomed back by the boss. I guess it was hard to find a diligent foreign worker like me who could exist in the boss's little kingdom. It was more humiliation, but it was part of being a man—sometimes you have to humble yourself to make a living.

He took some pleasure at chastising me over my invitation to come over for a visit, speaking to me like he was my kindergarten teacher.

"Bert, if I had gone over there when you invited me, I would be in prison," he said with glee. It was not exactly true, as the coup was attempted long after I invited him, but I got his point. As a prominent businessman, he could have been swept up in the wake of the failed coup. "You should have never left here," he continued, smiling. I needed the job, so I just smiled back.

I was now the foreigner of bad advice. My invitation for him to visit was added to a previous incident when I advised him to buy some local airline's stock when it was first issued. Somehow, I had obtained a special privilege to get it at a reduced rate. He did not buy, but almost immediately after the stock came out, Thailand experienced the Black May political protests and the stock fell precipitously, causing me similar embarrassment. I remember the boss chiding me about it and me feebly saying to him at the time, "Who would have thought they would just shoot all those people?" I resolved not to recommend anything to anyone again.

I still had enough ego left to be worried about what Andrew would say. He was right where I left him, in the school break room, going over student paperwork in his slow and deliberate way.

I had expected he would mock me for my inevitable return to teaching penury. But I found he had unexpectedly taken up drinking and was a bit disheveled.

When I caught him sneaking a drink from a hip flask with shaking hands, I asked, "Why are you doing this to yourself?"

"I have to do something with this life," he replied.

I would eventually tell him a modified version of my adventures, casting me as the virtuous hero at all points, as humans tend to do.

All Andrew said about it was, "You made a good mess over there."

I guess it was good he did not know the whole story, but he was impressed overall and that was good enough for me.

In time, all the things that happened and that could have happened returned to me. Sometimes, as I was in bed in the morning, in the moments before I had to get up, it would wash over me—the mistakes I made and the ones I could have made, and then the fear was greater than it ever had been at the time. I did not end up as I had started. They had made me pray.

It was back to teaching standardized entrance tests for U.S. universities to rich Thai kids. I went back to eating at the same food stall run by the lady who picked out the best fish for her customers each morning. She smiled at me still, not knowing what had happened and what I had done.

I rented a new room in my old apartment building in Bangkok. It was better than the last one I had and thankfully had a water heater. I tried to look on the bright side and relished taking a long hot shower. "A little water clears us of this deed," as was said.

I returned to my old rules—no motorcycles or boats, and no driving at night. But I don't know if it matters. A man still has to take a chance and I'm sure I will again.

Some people live, some people die—just so it is not me dying. This is probably not something to say out loud. One's own philosophy is not something others should know. I ran here and there because I could, because a world was created that was open to me.

Mike tracked me down; I do not know how. We had some beers at a pub. These days, I was experiencing the comfort that alcohol could give, its clarifying and calming effect. I tried not to drink too much. I told myself that this is what sometimes happens when you dare to be lucky—you end up looking at golden liquid in a glass most nights.

Mike asked me if I had heard from Ganju, but I had not. I said Ganju would surely find a way, and he and his warrior's ways would be okay.

Neither of us had heard anything about what happened to Tieng either, but Mike noted, "He's a big-time guy. He'll be fine."

"Tieng is a big-time guy while I'm back to teaching English," I replied.

We both laughed and drank some more.

Mike let slip that the secure radios and phones I had set up were not really secure. However, from my experience listening into the audio from the signal house, I had already suspected that just about any device was tappable—at least by the Americans who had made them. Years later, when a "high official" showed me one of these untappable phones in his home, I inwardly chuckled, knowing that the Americans could listen to every word he said, the poor third world fool.

Mike thought it hilarious when I told him the full story of getting my passport back and my escape. He was impressed by my luck. Mike had escaped the chaos via some vague method that involved the local military.

"They said I looked like something from their folklore—a golden prince who wore a black cloak to disguise himself," he explained.

I did not say anything in return. I could not tell exactly what he thought about this.

"It was a compliment, I think," he said, both with uncertainty and almost laughing.

I knew he did not want everything to be about something like this, yet it always was. Everything was as it always was.

That Mike had gotten out and then found me in Bangkok was no surprise. I never doubted he would. When I asked him who he really worked for, he said, "I don't work for anybody. Remember that. Nobody works for anybody." He smiled and took a swig of beer.

Not long after, Nick Leeson destroyed Barings Bank. He was around my age and unlucky. Between that and my own adventure, I wondered why I had not achieved something like him yet. I did not want to destroy a banking institution or destroy anything, really, but he had done something, even if it was for the worse. I had yet to achieve anything. At least I was willing to be lucky.

I still had the money from Chiang. I never declared it, and no one ever questioned or audited me. The money slowly got used up and one day I was back to where I was before and could not remember where it had gone.

I still had the prime minister's hairbrush that I took from his house. I suppose it was a strange and amazing thing to have—and hard to explain now to anyone why I had it. Maybe it is like those soldiers who took things at the end of a war— like allied soldiers who got Hitler's comb. It is what I have left from that time now—a dumb trophy.

I would be on eggshells for a few years, wondering if some paperwork was being cooked up—indicted back in that country for insurrection. But no, no one came after me. I was inconsequential.

It was easy not to matter. The history of that country proved it. I tested myself and came away with not much eventually, but that is the way of the world. I had gotten away with it and was a little smarter, that's all.

I returned to my old footpaths, moving from my apartment to the school through the alleyways of Bangkok. I passed the mute man at the temple, Dang, still forever sweeping. He would sometimes drift down the streets where I worked at the school, walking aimlessly.

One morning, as I was walking by, he suddenly veered towards me, stopping me in my path. He momentarily stood up straight, looked me in the eye, and said in perfectly accented English, "I worked for the CIA and look what they did to me!"

I was stunned. He had never spoken to me before. Everyone knew there was something wrong with him, like all the castoffs who lived at temples. Then, the moment passed, and Dang resumed his normal posture and went back to his sweeping.

When I told my boss at the school about this, he was so amused that he uncharacteristically laughed in my face. He told me that everyone knows this man and he never speaks, and, if he could speak, he would not speak English. I said that it really did happen, but he was contemptuous. "That is impossible," he said through his laughter.

It was probably just a random weird event, but it served for me as the end of my impossible adventure. I never heard Dang speak again, and, as far as I know, no one else did either. I do not know if this was connected to anything else or if anything really is.

I learned that the past followed me. It was now something in the world waiting for me, always waiting, pressing forward, forever nearing.

The doing of a thing was not the end of it, but the initiation of a thread that needed, wanted, desired, pleaded to be completed in some way. Almost making a mistake had more weight in the remembering than the mistakes actually made. It forced me wide awake and weary, and sometimes I could not lift my head off the pillow.

It made me recall Rangsei and what might have been between two people. I told myself that I have nothing for that, but I remembered telling her, "I think I knew you before in another life. When I was kissing you, I thought, I'm finally kissing you again." That was love, I guess. But just like thinking we had kissed before, love itself was a deception, and it faded away as the practical and solid world intervened.

I looked for Fon, my old girlfriend, but she was gone, and I never found her. The universe again made sure it wasn't easy.

In the end, I admitted that some things mattered, maybe Rangsei or Fon. Maybe something like that. What fools we are, and what a lucky fool I was, I admit.

If you ever hear I went crazy or committed suicide or that I came down with a sudden cancer, it is likely that... well, you know, they got to me like they did to Rangsei and Amnuay and Phong and Ganju, and even Thaw Kia and Chiang and crazy Dang at the temple. We challenged history but were not big enough, after all, to change the way things had to go. Everything tends to even out. The bigness and the history overwhelms. But you can try. And, as always, I deny everything.

**** **** ****

Bert Mars returns in a NEW ADVENTURE in *Edge of the Golden Moon*

RON MORRIS is a writer, political analyst, and traveler.

Books by Ron Morris

Edge of the Golden Moon

Matter of a Thing Absolute

In a Country with No Name

There Are Still Unknown Places

Last Century

The Thai Book: A Field Guide to Thai Political Motivations